Check into ████ for delightful tales of detection!

Room with a Clue
The view from the Pennyfoot's roof garden is lovely—but for Lady Eleanor Danbury, it was the last thing she ever saw. Now Cecily must find out who sent the snobbish society matron falling to her death . . .

Do Not Disturb
Mr. Bickley answered the door knocker and ended up dead. Cecily must capture the culprit—before murder darkens another doorstep . . .

Service for Two
Dr. McDuff's funeral became a fiasco when the mourners found a stranger's body in the casket. Now Cecily must close the case—for at the Pennyfoot, murder is a most unwelcome guest . . .

Eat, Drink, and Be Buried
April showers bring May flowers—when one of the guests is found strangled with a maypole ribbon. Soon the May Day celebration turns into a hotel investigation—and Cecily fears it's a merry month . . . for murder.

Check-Out Time
Life at the Pennyfoot hangs in the balance one sweltering summer when a distinguished guest plunges to his death from his top-floor balcony. Was it the heat . . . or cold-blooded murder?

Grounds for Murder
The Pennyfoot's staff was put on edge when a young gypsy was hacked to death in the woods near Badgers End. And now it's up to Cecily to find out who at the Pennyfoot has a deadly ax to grind . . .

Pay the Piper
The Pennyfoot's bagpipe contest ended on a sour note when one of the pipers was murdered. Cecily must catch the killer—before another piper pays for his visit with his life . . .

Chivalry Is Dead
The jousting competition had everyone excited, until someone began early by practicing on—and murdering—Cecily's footman. Now she must discover who threw the lethal lance . . .

Ring for Tomb Service
St. Bartholomew's Week is usually one of Cecily's favorite times of the year. But this year, the celebration is marred by the unholiest of acts—murder . . .

Death with Reservations
When the doctor claims food poisoning killed a Pennyfoot guest, Cecily is suspicious. She'll have to do some investigating of her own—before death becomes the special of the day . . .

MORE MYSTERIES FROM THE
BERKLEY PUBLISHING GROUP...

DYING ROOM ONLY

KATE KINGSBURY

BERKLEY PRIME CRIME, NEW YORK

DYING ROOM ONLY

A Berkley Prime Crime Book / published by arrangement with the author

PRINTING HISTORY
Berkley Prime Crime edition / October 1998

The Penguin Putnam Inc. World Wide Web site address is
http://www.penguinputnam.com

ISBN: 0-425-16568-X

Berkley Prime Crime Books are published
by The Berkley Publishing Group,
a member of Penguin Putnam Inc.,
375 Hudson Street, New York, NY 10014.
The name BERKLEY PRIME CRIME and the BERKLEY PRIME CRIME
design are trademarks belonging to Berkley Publishing Corporation.

PRINTED IN THE UNITED STATES OF AMERICA

10 9 8 7 6 5 4 3 2 1

DYING ROOM ONLY

CHAPTER

1

The Annual Spring Ball of 1910 promised to be the most prestigious night of the year for the Pennyfoot Hotel. The weather cooperated beautifully, providing a light refreshing breeze from the ocean and a remarkably mild temperature for the early spring evening.

The Esplanade, usually deserted at this time of the year, echoed with the clatter of hoofbeats and the creak of carriage springs, with an occasional pop and bang from one of those pesky motorcars that cluttered up the place with their noisy, smoky exhaust.

Watching from the window of the hotel drawing room, Phoebe Carter-Holmes felt immensely pleased with the attendance. Elegant ladies by the score, resplendent in pastel ball gowns glittering with sequins and with their flat-brimmed hats weighed down with an assortment of feathers, flowers, and lace, stepped gracefully out of carriages on the arms of their escorts.

Dressed in shiny top hats and immaculate black frock coats with pin-striped trousers, the gentlemen looked every bit as impressive as they assisted their companions up the white marble steps of the front entrance.

All in all, Phoebe thought, clasping her orchid kid-gloved hands in delight, this evening would appear to be an indisputable success. Obviously her magnificent feat of securing the appearance of the noted magician, the Great Denmarric himself, was about to pay off handsome dividends. Now just let Madeline Pengrath laugh at that.

Phoebe was responsible for all the entertainment at the Pennyfoot, and Madeline, who arranged the decor for the events, constantly cast aspersions on her efforts. Madeline would have a difficult time indeed finding fault with this assemblage, Phoebe thought with satisfaction.

As it happened, Madeline planned to attend the magician's performance that night, and Phoebe couldn't wait to flaunt her accomplishment in front of the sardonic woman.

"Blimey, that's a flipping big crowd out there tonight."

Phoebe started as her thoughts were interrupted by the harsh voice of Charlotte Watkins, who had just entered the drawing room. Normally Phoebe wouldn't be caught dead conversing with such a lowly creature.

Charlotte's face was caked with powder, and her cheeks highly rouged. Something disgusting had been painted around her eyes, making her look like a startled clown, and she reeked of rose water. Everyone knew that painted women were wicked and were to be avoided at all costs.

Charlotte nevertheless had to be afforded a reluctant respect, much against Phoebe's will. She would have much preferred to treat the harlot with the disdain she no doubt deserved. It was a regrettable misfortune, however, that Charlotte Watkins happened to be married to the Great Denmarric himself.

"It is indeed a good audience," Phoebe agreed stiffly. "Your husband must be exceptionally popular."

"He does all right." Charlotte shrugged in an unrefined

manner, making Phoebe cringe. The woman's stark white gown was quite vulgar, loaded down as it was with garish sequins and bugle beads. Phoebe was quite thankful that no one else was in the room to see her lower herself by conversing with this creature.

"I understand that several of his followers from Wellercombe are here to see him," she mumbled in an effort to appear sociable. She didn't want Charlotte complaining to her husband about the adverse treatment she'd received.

"Yeah, they really like his tricks, though they've seen them over and over enough times." Charlotte sniffed in a most uncouth manner. " 'Course, I've seen them all, too. But I still like to see 'em all again. Never missed a performance, I haven't."

"Really?" Phoebe murmured. "How terribly supportive of you."

Charlotte lifted her shoulders in that dreadful shrug again. "Well, I dunno about that. Dennis wants me to come so as I can help him with the props, like. See, Dennis don't let nobody else near his stuff except for his assistant. I used to be his assistant until we got married. Now he says it ain't proper for his wife to be on the stage with him. That's why he has Desiree help him instead of me."

Desiree, Phoebe thought, with a quiet huff of her breath. She knew better than that, of course. So did a good many people in the audience tonight. The magician's new assistant was none other than Ivy Glumm, who used to work as a waitress in Dolly's tea shop in the High Street.

In fact, it was more than likely that the local residents of Badgers End had come to the Pennyfoot more to ogle the downfall of a local girl they knew well, rather than any desire to watch a magician try to fool them with his magic tricks.

"Mind you," Charlotte was saying as she leaned forward to peer out of the window, "Desiree's not much better than his last assistant. I don't know where he finds them, honest

I don't. They don't have no class nowadays, if you know what I mean.''

Phoebe emphatically did know.

Charlotte straightened again. "If you ask me, the old fool doesn't want me up there with him because he thinks I'm too flipping old for the job. Can you imagine that? And me nearly twenty years younger than him?''

To Phoebe's horror, the despicable creature actually had the audacity to nudge her shoulder with a bony elbow. She moved away and flicked at the offending spot with her gloved fingers. "Well, I'm sure he is grateful for your help, nonetheless. Actually I feel quite envious of all his props. As you know, I put on several spectaculars a year here at the hotel, and I would dearly love to be in possession of some of the magician's equipment. That huge props basket on wheels, for instance. How much easier it would be to transport everything in that.''

"Well, he has to have that, don't he? We'd never get everything back and forth across the stage otherwise.'' Charlotte looked hopefully at the door. "I don't suppose Mrs. Sinclair will be popping in here before the show?''

Phoebe fervently hoped not. "I really couldn't say.''

"I'd like to meet her.'' Charlotte tugged on her wrinkled gloves. "I've never met a woman what owned an hotel before. What's she like?''

Phoebe lifted her chin. "Cecily Sinclair is a charming, sophisticated, and gracious woman. She does a wonderful job of running the Pennyfoot Hotel and its staff, and she is highly respected by every one of them.''

Charlotte seemed singularly unimpressed. "Must seem strange, though, having a woman for a boss. Someone told me her husband left her the hotel when he died.''

"Really,'' Phoebe murmured, determined not to be drawn into gossip about her dear friend.

"Her manager helps her a lot, thought, don't he?''

"I do believe so,'' Phoebe said haughtily, though she couldn't imagine what business it was of this awful woman.

"You reckon he's sweet on her?" Charlotte asked slyly.

Phoebe held onto her temper by a slim margin. "Mr. Baxter is a respectable gentleman with impeccable manners. He is also an employee of Mrs. Sinclair's. He would not presume to step above his station."

Actually Baxter was now a full partner in the hotel. Phoebe saw no need, however, to enlighten Charlotte Watkins of that fact.

Charlotte's eyes narrowed. "That's not what I heard."

Deciding that her obligation to the Great Denmarric's wife only went so far, Phoebe said briskly, "Oh, my, look at the time. I really must run. I have to be in the ballroom to supervise the stagehands."

"Just so long as you don't touch Dennis's props," Charlotte said with a lurid wink. "Magicians don't like people getting near their stuff. They guard their secrets like they was the Crown Jewels."

"I'll remember," Phoebe assured her. Personally she had no desire to touch anything that belonged to Denmarric or his wife, she thought, as she hurried down to the ballroom.

Minutes later she had forgotten about her distaste as she watched the magician perform his miraculous tricks. She had chosen a spot in front of the door that led to the wings and had a clear view of everything happening onstage.

She would have preferred to watch from the wings themselves. Denmarric had given explicit orders, however, that no one, absolutely no one, was to be allowed in the wings or backstage during the performance unless given express permission.

Denmarric's assistant, Desiree, as she called herself, seemed nervous in spite of her recent successful Christmas season with the magician at the Wellercombe Hippodrome. She scuttled about the stage with a grim smile fixed firmly in place and jumped whenever Denmarric barked an order.

The girl was painfully thin, with absolutely no hips or bosom at all which, in Phoebe's opinion, was just as well, since her pale blue costume was quite scandalous. Even the trimmings of sparkling silver sequins couldn't detract from the fact that there was more skin than fabric on display.

At one point Desiree dropped a metal decanter as she was handing it to the magician, and Phoebe saw quite clearly his fierce scowl before he wiped it off and smiled for the benefit of the audience.

Not a man to be crossed, Phoebe thought, beginning to feel sorry for Ivy. When the girl had worked at Dolly's, she'd at least had some spirit. Although Phoebe had never cared for her personally, she didn't like to see a woman cowed by a man in such a drastic way.

The incident must have unnerved Desiree, as a few minutes later Denmarric stepped forward to center stage and announced he would present his assistant with a beautiful dove. What actually emerged from his pocket, however, was a very agitated duck, who pecked viciously at the magician's hand as he carried the squawking bird off-stage amid much laughter.

Only Phoebe, from her position at the edge of the stage, saw the sharp cuff across the face that Denmarric gave his assistant before he strode back onstage with a good-humored smile.

Phoebe would have liked to give the man a piece of her mind, but soon his magic enthralled her again, and she had to marvel at his dexterity as he produced flowers, scarves, and even a cake adorned with lighted candles apparently from thin air.

Each trick became more ambitious as the evening wore on, producing louder gasps and even a shriek or two as well as thunderous applause. It was all music to Phoebe's ears. She would have loved to see Madeline's face, had she known where she was sitting, but it was difficult to see the audience with the gaslights turned down.

Her triumph would have to wait until the committee meeting the next day. She, Madeline, and Cecily were to meet in the hotel library to discuss plans for the next tea dance. She could enjoy her moment of glory then, Phoebe decided.

Denmarric came to the end of his latest trick and held up his hand. An expectant hush fell over the ballroom as a low roll of drums announced something spectacular. The lights dimmed onstage, except for two single spotlights, one on Denmarric, the other on his quivering assistant.

"Now, ladies and gentlemen," Denmarric announced in his booming voice, "I am about to perform what amounts to a miracle. A sight such as you have never seen in your life before. A death-defying trick that will amaze you, astound you, and astonish you. A feat that could only be performed by the one and only, the Great Denmarric!"

With a flourish of his swirling black cape, the magician stalked to the edge of the stage where two large boxes on wheels had stood throughout the performance. Stepping behind one of them, he pushed the container to the rear center of the stage and positioned it in front of the curtains that served as a backdrop.

Watched closely by a fascinated audience, he then crossed the stage again to the second box and brought it back to front center stage. "Ladies and gentlemen!" he cried, having secured the full attention of his audience, most of whom no doubt were panting with anticipation, "I will now present the world-famous feat that has everyone in the entire universe completely baffled. Please pay attention to this box."

With a flamboyant flourish, he threw open the door of the box. It looked rather like a primitive wardrobe inside, Phoebe decided, somewhat disappointed. She had expected something a little more elaborate and decorative than a plain box with three bare walls and a door.

"I am going to put my beautiful assistant into this box," Denmarric announced, "which, as you can plainly see for yourselves, is just an ordinary, quite empty box. Then, ladies and gentlemen, I will close the door, and behold, Desiree will vanish into thin air!"

Several gasps greeted this startling announcement. Phoebe could actually feel the excitement rippling through the audience. Why, she was shivering with it herself. This indeed was to be her crowning glory. At last she had succeeded in a triumphant presentation that would be difficult to surpass.

That last thought somewhat dampened her enthusiasm, but just then Desiree stepped forward and dropped a deep curtsey, the effect of which was quite lost, in Phoebe's opinion, because of her scanty costume.

The drumroll intensified, raising the avid expectations of the audience. Desiree pranced up to the box, sent a little wave of farewell to the spectators, and stepped inside. There was barely enough room for her elbows as she stood with her arms clamped at her sides.

"Now," Denmarric bellowed gamely above the thundering drums, "I will close the doors, and Desiree will disappear. Before your very eyes, ladies and gentlemen!"

He slammed the door shut. The drums ceased immediately, and a tense silence settled over the ballroom. Phoebe's skin tingled as she stood stock-still, terrified to make a sound and draw attention to herself.

Denmarric sounded unusually loud, even though he'd lowered his voice. "Ladies and gentlemen, before I open the door again, I will attempt to prove my confidence in my ability to perform this marvelous feat." Once more the drums began to quietly roll.

Phoebe watched in breathless silence as the magician strode to a table and grasped a sword. Loud gasps echoed throughout the room as the light gleamed on its vicious blade. Denmarric brandished the sword in the air, then advanced upon the box.

The magician touched the tip of the sword to the side of the box, then, with a dramatic gesture, plunged the blade through the heart of the narrow compartment.

Phoebe uttered a little squeak, her delicate stomach protesting as she stared in horror, fully expecting a river of blood to run across the stage.

Again and again the magician plunged the sword into the box, until finally he was satisfied. The murmurs died down again as he laid down the sword and approached the door.

"Now, ladies and gentlemen, we shall see if Desiree survived." The drumbeats rolled relentlessly as he threw open the door.

Phoebe felt quite weak with relief. The box was quite empty. How this amazing man had done it she didn't know, for it would have been impossible for Desiree to leave the box without being seen. For the moment, however, she was awfully glad the trick had succeeded.

The audience was in full agreement, apparently, as they applauded and cheered for a full minute, until the magician held up his hand.

"Now, ladies and gentlemen, we come to the most difficult part of this amazing trick. We must bring Desiree back from her journey to the black beyond. I must ask you all to concentrate, since I shall need your help for this incredible feat."

Phoebe obediently closed her eyes. Since this meant she couldn't see what was going on, she just as quickly opened them again. She saw Denmarric push the box across to the edge of the stage and carefully position it. Leaving it there, he crossed the stage to the other side, with the gaze of the entire audience watching his every move.

There he paused and faced the hushed spectators. "Now, ladies and gentlemen, let us all concentrate. Please, close your eyes for a moment if it will help you to focus your mind. We must use every ounce of willpower to bring Desiree back from the clutches of those who would hold her."

Silence settled over the audience. The magician stood with bowed head for several seconds, then slowly raised his hand. As he did so, the eerie silence was suddenly shattered by the shocking sound of a woman's high-pitched, hysterical laughter.

For a moment Phoebe froze, outraged by this insolent intrusion. An uneasy murmuring ran through the crowd, while Denmarric merely stood, staring in the direction of the wings, seemingly confused by the interruption.

The sound ceased abruptly, the sudden silence almost as shocking as the laughter had been. Denmarric shook his head, as if to clear his mind.

Phoebe didn't wait to hear what he said. The sound had come from the wings, after she had issued strict instructions that with the exception of Denmarric's stagehands, no one be allowed in the area. Phoebe did not like her orders disobeyed. She intended to seek out the perpetrator and give the woman a well-aimed piece of her mind.

Furious at this despicable attempt to sabotage what had promised to be her biggest success, Phoebe opened the door and headed for the wings.

CHAPTER

❈ 2 ❈

From her vantage point in the balcony, Cecily Sinclair had a full view of the stage. She had been following the entire performance with great interest, since she and Baxter had once met Denmarric after a performance at the Hippodrome in Wellercombe.

She found the magician's performance fascinating, a view hardly shared by Baxter, however. He still hadn't recovered from the embarrassment of being mistaken for a newspaper cameraman by the acerbic magician, who had then more or less thrown both Baxter and Cecily out of his dressing room.

Seated next to Cecily this evening, Baxter had sat through the magician's entire performance with a stoic expression, implying that he was only suffering through the ordeal in order to please her.

When the sound of the shrill laughter echoed along the balcony, Cecily thought at first that it was part of the act.

But then Denmarric paused, staring off stage with an odd look on his face, and Cecily knew he was as startled as the rest of the audience.

A flash of light next to the stage caught her eye, and she saw Phoebe slip through the door to the wings, closing it behind her.

"What the devil was that?" Baxter whispered, leaning forward to get a better look.

"I don't know. It sounded like someone laughing."

"I've never heard anyone laugh like that before," Baxter muttered. "It sounded almost insane."

"I think it was because it echoed across the stage," Cecily said, watching the magician as he turned back to the audience.

"Ladies and gentlemen," Denmarric announced in his booming voice, "I must apologize for the interruption. Now I must ask you to once again concentrate, as I attempt to bring Desiree back from the living dead."

"A contradiction in terms, if I ever heard one," Baxter muttered.

Cecily wasn't really listening. She was wondering if Phoebe had caught up with whoever had emitted that ghastly sound.

Phoebe, in fact, had almost succumbed to a disaster of her own. While rounding the corner backstage, she'd narrowly missed being run over by the huge props basket, pushed by a surly young stagehand in a checkered cap. He brushed right by her, completely ignoring her breathless apology.

Such an ignorant person, she thought as she hurried through to the wings. What were the young people coming to these days? But then these theatrical louts were inclined to be outlandish, not like respectable people, that was for certain.

Reaching the wings, Phoebe paused for breath, clutching her lace-covered throat with her gloved hand. Denmarric appeared to have recovered from the interruption and was about to perform his moment of triumph.

Pleased that she was not going to miss one of the highlights of the show after all, Phoebe watched with bated breath as Denmarric stalked across to where the second box waited at the rear of center stage.

"Ladies and gentlemen," the magician's voice boomed, "you have all seen with your own eyes Desiree step into that box over there and disappear. I will now bring her back, and to prove that she did indeed vanish from your sight, I will transport her into this box over here, which as you all know, has stood empty throughout the entire performance. Now keep your eyes on this box, ladies and gentlemen, as I open the door and give you . . . Desiree!"

Phoebe craned forward for a better view as the magician threw open the door. Several members of the audience gasped, and then once more murmurs rippled throughout the ballroom.

From where she stood, Phoebe could not see into the box. She could see Denmarric's face quite clearly though. He had his back to the audience and was making no attempt to hide his thunderstruck expression.

Her heart sank. Surely, *surely,* something hadn't gone wrong with the trick? Denmarric couldn't possibly have failed, could he? He had such a wonderful reputation. Yet it was obvious that something was terribly amiss, since Desiree had not stepped out of the box.

Still staring at the magician, who was now closing the door again, she started when someone spoke her name from behind her. She jerked her head around so fast that she dislodged wisps of the large pink plume that adorned her hat. They floated unnoticed to the floor as she stared at Cecily. "What happened?" she asked urgently. "Has something happened to Desiree?"

"I really don't know," Cecily said, looking somewhat concerned. "The box was quite empty."

"Oh, my." Phoebe clutched her throat again. "You

don't think she's still floating around with the living dead, do you?'' Realizing what she'd just said, she uttered a shrill laugh to cover up her embarrassment. ''Listen to me, will you? I sound just like Madeline. I've been listening to her hocus-pocus for too long, that's quite plain to see.''

''I think that something went amiss with the trick,'' Cecily said, positioning herself so that she could see onto the stage. ''The question is, where is Desiree now?''

''Perhaps the Great Denmarric has an even more spectacular way of bringing her back, and this is all just part of the act,'' Phoebe suggested, not too hopefully.

Cecily didn't answer her. She seemed preoccupied, her attention fully on the magician.

Phoebe just couldn't bring herself to accept the fact that Denmarric could have suffered such an indisputable failure on her special night. He had not only let himself down, he had failed her as well, and if he could not redeem himself in the next few minutes or so, she was not prepared to forgive him.

She glared at the offending magician as he faced the audience, his expression once more smoothly bland. ''Ladies and gentlemen,'' he announced, his voice only slightly subdued, ''it would seem as though Desiree is not destined to come back just yet. I do, however, have a charming assistant waiting in the wings who, I'm sure, will be happy to assist me for the remainder of the performance. I give you my beautiful wife, Charlotte, ladies and gentlemen.''

A polite scattering of applause greeted this announcement as Charlotte, looking quite different in a sparkling red costume, entered from the opposite side of the stage to where Phoebe stood with Cecily.

It was obvious the audience was confused. Even though Denmarric succeeded in levitating his wife several inches above the seats of the two chairs where she had previously rested, the expectant silence that had greeted the magician's previous tricks was no longer evident. Instead, hushed whispers and not-so-quiet muttering could be heard throughout the room.

Phoebe felt quite sick as she surveyed the ruins of her triumph. Just once, just one time, she would like to organize an evening of entertainment without something or someone sabotaging the entire project. It just wasn't fair.

At last the magician and his wife took their final bows, and the curtains closed to a respectable round of applause, though falling far short of the acclaim Phoebe had expected.

Cecily still offered no comment. Her gaze was firmly fixed on Denmarric, who barely waited for the curtains to meet before spinning on his heel to head for the original casket in front of the wings.

Phoebe stood just a few feet from the box from which Desiree had disappeared. She could see the rivulets of perspiration carving little white paths through the dark stage makeup the magician wore as he opened the door of the box and stepped inside.

He closed the door behind him, and Phoebe suffered several moments of anxiety until he reappeared. Then, followed by Charlotte, who was saying something urgent to him in a low tone, he hurried to the second box and again disappeared inside it.

A minute or two later he stepped out and looked helplessly at his wife. Cecily muttered something under her breath and hurried out on stage, followed closely by Phoebe, who was not about to miss a single iota of this annoying episode.

Denmarric turned to Cecily as she reached him. He dipped his head in a slight bow, then said heavily, "My apologies, Mrs. Sinclair. Something has gone terribly wrong. My assistant seems to have disappeared."

"Isn't that what she was supposed to do?" Phoebe snapped irritably. She wasn't about to let the inept fool off lightly. She didn't have Cecily's patience when it came to sheer incompetence.

The magician allowed Phoebe a withering glance. "Indubitably, madam. Under the circumstances, I would suggest that I was a little too successful. At this point I am at a loss as to the whereabouts of my assistant.''

''H'in that case,'' a pompous voice announced from the wings, ''I would suggest that you not touch anything until the constabulary 'ave 'ad a chance to h'inspect it all.''

''Oh, Lord,'' Cecily muttered, looking quite ill. ''P.C. Northcott. Here comes even more trouble.''

''What do you think bleeding 'appened to her, then?'' Gertie demanded as she struggled to prize the cap off the milk churn the next morning. ''She couldn't disappear just like that, could she?''

The young man seated at the scrubbed table in the center of the hotel's spacious kitchen lifted his head. ''I don't see why not. After all, the bloke's a magician. He's supposed to make things disappear.''

Gertie straightened her back and thrust a strand of dark hair out of her eyes with her fist. ''He's supposed to bloody well bring her back again, ain't he? Mark my words, Samuel, there's something blinking strange going on there.''

Samuel shrugged. ''Magicians are strange people. It's probably a publicity stunt, done to get his name in the papers. What with the summer season coming up, he can probably use the attention.'' He took a bite out of the Cornish pasty that Mrs. Chubb, the housekeeper, always had ready for him in the mornings.

''Shouldn't think he'd want people to know he'd bloody messed up a trick.'' Gertie bent over the churn to have another go at the stubborn cap.

''It was a crummy night anyway,'' Samuel muttered, ''what with all the traffic. I've never seen so many carriages. It was a right flipping mess, I can tell you.''

''It's always a mess out there on events night.'' Gertie grunted as she pried the cap around.

''What made it worse, some of the buggers didn't want to wait for me to bring their carriages around. Ho, no.''

Samuel uttered a disdainful laugh. "No, they has to get them themselves, don't they? Caused an even bigger bloody mess than usual. I sometimes wonder what the heck I'm doing wasting me life as a blinking stable manager."

The cap twisted in Gertie's hands, and she heaved a sigh of relief. Her back was breaking after she'd bent over the bleeding thing all that time. "You like being a stable manager. You're just fed up because Doris is going to London for an audition on the Variety stage. You're afraid she'll get blinking lucky and you won't bloody see her no more."

"Don't make no difference to me what she does. It's her life." Samuel finished the last mouthful of his Cornish pasty and got to his feet. Brushing the crumbs from his shirt, he muttered, "Anyhow, I've got to get back to the stables. If I don't keep an eye on the lads out there, they won't clean the traps properly, and then there'll be hell to pay from madam."

Gertie laughed. "I wouldn't blinking worry about madam. She's got her hands full trying to find that poor sod what disappeared."

"More'n likely she's run off to the Smoke to look for fame and fortune, like everyone else around here." Samuel reached the door just as a young, fresh-faced girl wearing a too-large apron and crisp white cap burst into the kitchen.

"Oops, sorry," Doris said breathlessly. "Didn't see you standing there, Samuel."

"That's all right, Bright Eyes. I'd be happy to have you bump into me any time." He gave her a cheeky grin and disappeared through the door.

"Oo, hark at him," Doris muttered as she carried the tray she was holding over to the sink. "Thinks he's Mr. Marvelous, don't he?"

"He likes you a lot," Gertie said quietly. She felt sort of sorry for Samuel. Everyone knew he was sweet on Doris, but all she had in her head was her silly dream of becoming a Variety star.

"Well, I like him, too." Doris dropped the silverware

into the sink with a loud clatter. "That doesn't mean I like him hanging around me all the time. He knows I've got me heart set on meeting a toff. I'm not going to waste me time on a stable manager, now am I?" Crossing over to the stove, she dragged a huge cauldron of steaming water off the top and hauled it over to the sink.

"If you really like someone, you shouldn't care about what they bleeding do for a living." Gertie fingered the letter nestled in the pocket of her apron. It had arrived just that morning, and she'd only had time to read it once.

"I don't really like Samuel . . . not in that way." Doris sighed. "He's very nice, and I know he cares about me, but I'm going to be a big star and I'll meet all sorts of toffs. If Samuel's hanging around me, he's going to spoil me chances, ain't he."

"Just because you've got a bleeding audition with a London producer, it don't mean you're going to be a flipping star all at once. It might take you years to get well known. They could be bloody lonely years while you're waiting for your flipping toff what might not come along anyway. You'd do better to grab what's blinking offered now, if you ask me."

"I'd rather wait, thank you." Doris tossed her head, something she never did before she got the letter from the famous Variety singer, Bella DelRay, telling her about the audition.

Now, it seemed, the young housemaid was putting on airs and graces, just because some big shot in London promised to listen to her sing. Gertie didn't care for anyone what pretended to be what they wasn't. "What does Daisy say about all this?" she asked, her words ending in a grunt as she poured milk from the churn into a large china jug.

Daisy was Doris's twin and nanny to Gertie's twin babies. They all lived at the hotel, which worked out nicely for Gertie. But now that Doris could be on her way to a job in London, Gertie couldn't help wondering if her twin would go with her, leaving her with two very active toddlers to look after, as well as her exhausting job.

As chief housemaid she was kept running all day long and half the night. She wouldn't have time to be a good mother, too. All in all, Gertie thought glumly, things at the Pennyfoot looked as if they were about to change all over.

She dumped the churn back on the floor and carried the jug into the pantry. At least she had something to look forward to. Her fingers strayed to the letter in her pocket.

She'd been writing to Ross McBride for a few months now. Ever since she'd met him, the time he'd come to Badgers End for a bagpipes contest, she'd wondered if she'd done the right thing by sending him away.

She hadn't heard from him in ages; then a few months ago he'd written to her, and she'd written back. Now his letters arrived every few days or so, and each one more exciting than the last.

She got squiggles in her stomach every time she thought about him. She'd almost forgotten what he looked like, but not quite. She still remembered the way his eyes laughed at her, all twinkling and warm, and how his voice always made her knees weak.

She was looking forward very much to seeing Ross McBride again one day. Her stomach did a little jump at the thought. Maybe things weren't so bad after all.

Maybe Doris wouldn't get the job in London and would go on working at the Pennyfoot. Maybe that magician's assistant would turn up again, and it didn't mean more bad luck for the hotel, like everyone was saying.

And maybe, just maybe, some day something really special would come out of Ross McBride's letters.

CHAPTER
❦ 3 ❦

There were some mornings in Colonel Fortescue's life when he had great difficulty in regaining full consciousness. He'd been up and dressed for two hours and had consumed a gargantuan breakfast of fried salmon roe, smoked haddock and poached eggs, ham, sausage, liver, bacon, fried potatoes, fried tomatoes, and fried bread, followed by apple crumble and fresh cream.

The colonel had washed it all down with a couple of gin fizzes and several cups of heavily sweetened tea, all of which did little to alleviate the weight of his eyelids. His normally rapid blinking—a condition brought on by his narrow skirmishes with gunfire in the Boer War—had slowed down to a languorous flapping of his eyelashes instead.

In fact, so torpid did he feel, he was almost obliged to retire to his room for a nap, which was not his custom at all. Colonel Fortescue avoided naps like the plague. On the rare occasion he had taken one during the day, he had slept for several hours and had completely missed not only a meal, but his customary tipple at the bar beforehand.

Food the colonel could go without, but to deny himself the pleasure of his full count of liquor was to render him sleepless that night, thereby upsetting his entire schedule. For days afterward he'd fall asleep in the afternoon, missing out on more brandy and depriving himself of his sleep at night. A vicious circle, all told, that was to be avoided at all costs.

Ambling along the hallway in the direction of the foyer, Fortescue considered his options. The weather was nice—quite warm in fact, for the end of April. Perhaps a saunter in the rose garden might help to resuscitate his energy. He might even have the good fortune to bump into Phoebe Carter-Holmes again. The colonel smiled fondly as he stepped out into the dazzling sunlight. Although it had been six months or more since the pleasant encounter in the rose garden with Phoebe, he still remembered that good lady lying flat on her back on the grass while he administered his favorite remedy for all ills—straight gin.

Ever since that day, he fancied that Phoebe looked upon him with a more favorable eye. True, he hadn't actually come close enough to her to remind her of their shared adventure; she always seemed to be in such a blasted hurry. If he didn't know better, the colonel thought as he strolled toward the rose garden, he'd believe she was deliberately avoiding him.

He did know better, of course. The woman was merely showing admirable restraint. After all, she was the mother of the parish vicar and could not afford to frolic publicly with an unattached gentleman, no matter how innocent the encounter.

Fortescue sighed and twirled his mustache. Damn shame that. He would have enjoyed a romp in the hay with the old girl. True, having already buried one husband, she was not exactly the innocent charmer he once chased in his youth, but one could do a lot worse nowadays, with all this talk of emancipated women.

Phoebe Carter-Holmes was of the old school. She knew her place, by Jove, and she could still turn a pretty ankle when she set her mind to it. Yes, the colonel silently asserted, one could do a lot worse indeed.

Having reached that pleasant conclusion, he gazed around at his surroundings. He'd reached the rose garden without realizing it. And no wonder. Fortescue stared at the arbor in astonishment.

The trellis arch, which had once groaned under the weight of fragrant blossoms, now stood stark and bare. Dried-up branches trailed dismally down its sides, with no more than one or two anemic rosebuds to carry on the tradition.

In fact, the more Fortescue looked, the more shocked he became. The bushes, once neatly pruned and covered in glorious blooms, now stood forlorn and forsaken, their precious buds shriveling on the stems.

He'd almost forgotten about the death of John Thimble, the hotel gardener, who had been brutally struck down last summer by a demented guest at the Pennyfoot.

Fortescue shook his head at the pathetic sight of the once-majestic rose garden. He had never realized how much work John had put into the grounds of the hotel until now. By the looks of it, if Mrs. Sinclair didn't hire a new gardener post haste, there wouldn't be any bushes left to tend.

Turning his back on the depressing sight, Fortescue decided to head for the hills. Or rather, the cliffs overlooking the bay and the village of Badgers End. It had been many months since he had taken the short cut across the cliffs to the local pub. A couple of nasty experiences up there had rather put him off, and it was much easier just to have Samuel drive him down to the George and Dragon in the trap.

This morning, however, being such a bright, warm,

sunny day, he would take his stout cane and once more ramble over Putney Downs to the pub for his midday double gin and his pint of bitter chaser.

Having settled that, Fortescue went back to his room to retrieve his cane, then set out with a modest stride for the Downs. He didn't like to set too fast a pace at first. Invariably whenever he drew closer to the pub, his step quickened, and if he didn't take heed, he'd be at a fast trot by the time he reached his objective.

Which would be quite all right, if it wasn't for the fact that he'd be so out of breath he couldn't give his order. Dashed awkward that.

Striding out with returning vigor, the colonel climbed the grassy slopes to the Downs. The wind ruffled his beard, and the salty air filled his lungs as he trudged along the path at the edge of the cliffs. Seagulls swooped low, hoping for a tidbit, then, disappointed, glided out over the ocean for more fruitful prey.

He could see the smoke rising from the chimney stacks in the thatched roofs of the cottages across the bay, while the water sparkled with a thousand shimmering drops of sunlight. It was all very pleasant. Very pleasant indeed.

Until he heard the dog.

The mournful howl sent chills chasing down his back. The poor blighter must be hurt, he thought, marching faster now as if to outrun the pitiful sound. Surely its master would hear it and come to its rescue.

Fortescue did his best to shut out the awful noise. He concentrated on the sight and the smell of a full glass of beer topped with a thick collar of foam. He could taste it already, flowing over his lips and down his throat—cool, wet, and soothing after the burning gin.

Once more the unearthly howl rented the air, and Fortescue's stride faltered. No man worth his salt could ignore such a heart-wrenching plea. The colonel had seen many a man in the throes of death and had hardened himself to the sight, but he had never been able to watch an animal suffering without writhing in an agony of remorse.

He would never sleep at night if he left an animal to die in pain. Better to go put the poor bastard out of its misery. Taking a stern grip of his heavy cane, he changed direction and headed for the woods.

It took him several minutes to find the dog. The howling seemed to echo all around him, bouncing off trees and rippling through the bushes. The dark, damp interior of the woodland seemed to reach out clammy fingers to touch him while prickly nettles and thick, trailing blackberry vines waited to claw at his legs and trip him up.

He came upon the dog suddenly, while stepping over some fallen timber. It sat on its haunches, its black head raised to the sky, its jaws stretched open to emit the appalling howl.

Fortescue peered closer at it, keeping his distance at first. He knew only too well the danger of approaching an animal in pain. He called out softly, taking care to keep the cane hidden behind him. "Here, boy. Here, then! What's the matter, old chap?"

At the sound of his voice the terrible yowl cut off abruptly, leaving a deathly silence that was almost as unnerving. Fortescue stared—not at the dog, but what lay in front of it. Even as his mind accepted what he was looking at, the dog whined, then slunk away with its tail between its legs.

The colonel's eyelids began fluttering up and down like the frantic wings of a trapped moth. He inched forward, trying not to remember what he'd eaten for breakfast. The hand that he saw protruding from the hole was covered in dirt. Even so, he knew it was a woman. Or rather, it had been a woman.

He drew close enough to look down at the hole. Apparently the dog had been digging, no doubt curious about what lay buried there. The rest of the body was still covered in the moist, fresh-smelling earth. Very slowly, Fortescue bent down and brushed some of it away.

The light caught the glint of silver sequins, sparkling against a pale blue material. The colonel straightened in a hurry. He'd seen those sequins just the night before, adorning the skinny figure of Desiree, the Great Denmarric's assistant.

"I really cannot believe that a man of Mr. Denmarric's reputation could be careless enough to lose his assistant." Phoebe fussily settled herself on her customary chair at the left of the long Jacobean table.

"I rather doubt that Ivy's disappearance was the fault of the magician," Cecily said mildly. She had been hoping that the subject wouldn't come up. The weekly meeting of the entertainments committee was already late in beginning, and the third member of the committee, Madeline Pengrath, had not as yet put in an appearance.

Discussion on the unfortunate incident last night was bound to take up time that could be better spent on the details of the upcoming tea dance.

She watched Phoebe rest her parasol against the leg of the table, then straighten her enormous hat with a firm tug. The room felt cool, in spite of the flames leaping in the marble fireplace.

The library was Cecily's favorite room in the hotel. With its subdued paneling and floor-to-ceiling shelves crammed with books, its calm, restful atmosphere helped to soothe her troubled thoughts.

"Well, I'd like to know whose fault it is, in that case." Phoebe ran her fingers up her elbow-length gray gloves to smooth out the wrinkles. "After all, if the man puts a woman into a box, he should at least be capable of getting her out again. He's certainly not the magician I thought he was."

"That's what comes of dabbling in the devil's work," a soft, languid voice said from the doorway.

"Oh, there you are, Madeline." Cecily smiled at the delicate creature who seemed to float across the carpet in a cloud of cream gauze. Although Madeline's frocks were handsewn and of simple design, she always managed to impart an air of carefree elegance.

Her clothes and her dark, unbound hair reflected her personality—unusual, free-spirited, and more than a little mysterious. Many of the villagers in Badgers End considered her a witch, and there was no doubt that Madeline possessed some unique talents.

Cecily paid little heed to the whispers, though she had to admit there had been times when even she had been unsettled by Madeline's uncanny ability to sense what was beyond the grasp of mere mortals.

"Devil's work!" Phoebe repeated, sounding aghast. "I hardly consider the Great Denmarric an evil man. A magician is nothing more than a skillful manipulator, that is all. Denmarric's performance can in no way be confused with your witchcraft."

"Really?" Madeline sank onto her chair and curled an arm over the back of it. "Then what do you make of poor Desiree's disappearing act? I'd say that transcends the boundaries of manipulation, wouldn't you, Cecily?"

Knowing full well that Madeline was attempting to mock Phoebe, Cecily refused to rise to the bait. She was quite sure that once she allowed the two women to engage in their usual militant exchange, it would take an army of generals to pry them apart.

"What I would like to know," Phoebe said, hunting in her sleeve for her handkerchief, "is who was responsible for that hideous laughter right in the middle of Mr. Denmarric's act. It was no wonder he lost his concentration. Apparently whoever she was, she also vanished without a trace, since I saw no one backstage, and she would have had to pass right by me to leave the wings."

Madeline yawned. "It was most likely Ivy laughing at the thought of Denmarric's face when he opened up the box and found it empty."

"Are you saying she deliberately walked out on him?"

Phoebe looked as if she were about to choke. "But I would have seen her leave the wings if that had been so."

"She could have remained hidden until we all left."

"But that's utterly contemptible. How could Ivy embarrass the poor man that way?"

Madeline's expression hardened. "From what I've heard, Denmarric is well known for ill-treating his assistants. Perhaps Ivy became tired of the abuse and decided to pay him back. If so, she certainly chose an effective way of doing so."

Phoebe shifted uncomfortably on her chair. "Yes, well, if that's so, I wouldn't want to be in her shoes when Mr. Denmarric meets up with her again. Even so, I consider her behavior despicable. Ivy Glumm ruined my presentation, and I shan't forgive her."

"Perhaps we should wait until we know exactly what happened before we lay the blame," Cecily said, anticipating Madeline's rejoinder. "Now, if I may change the subject, I'd like to know the details of your presentation at the tea dance this weekend, Phoebe."

"I'd like to know how we are going to hold a tea dance in the ballroom, now that P.C. Northcott refuses to let Mr. Denmarric remove his props from the stage. Half the area we normally use is roped off with a guard standing over it." Phoebe sniffed delicately. "I fail to see how any of that will help to find out what happened to Ivy Glumm."

"I'm sure that once the constable has inspected everything, the magician will be collecting his property," Cecily assured her, hoping she was right about that. "He must be as anxious to retrieve it as we are to be rid of it. In any case, we must plan the tea dance with that assumption."

Phoebe sighed. "Well, now, let me see. I thought, since this is an afternoon presentation, I should do something light. So I've acquired the services of a young woman who is very proficient on the piano. She also sings, I believe."

Madeline raised her eyebrows. "How very dull. Whatever happened to your performing snakes and dancing monkeys? Pray don't tell me you have lost your knack of discovering unique and scintillating entertainment?"

Phoebe, looking greatly surprised, fanned herself with her lace-edged handkerchief. "Why, thank you, Madeline. Most kind of you, I'm sure. I hadn't realized you appreciated my efforts."

Madeline smiled sweetly. "One could hardly ignore them, Phoebe, dear. I still fondly remember the abandon with which our elegant ladies dropped senseless into the arms of their escorts at the sight of your python writhing around on stage. And who could forget the screams when one of your sword dancers tried her best to plunge her weapon into the heart of Lady Dappleby?"

Phoebe's face turned bright pink. "Unfortunate accidents happen to the best of us. Such as last night. I'm quite sure that had the Great Denmarric not misplaced his assistant, his performance would have been talked about for weeks."

"There I fear you are wrong, Phoebe." Madeline swept back a handful of hair from her shoulder. "It is the unexpected and disastrous elements of your presentations that make them the most talked-about subject in Badgers End."

Phoebe sniffed. "Really. I was under the distinct impression that it was your hocus-pocus that caused the most gossip."

Cecily raised her hand. "Ladies, please. I would really like to know what kind of floral arrangements you will use for the tea dance, Madeline."

"And I would really like to know what happened to Ivy Glumm," Phoebe said crossly. "I'm getting a little weary of bearing the brunt of others' mistakes. Someone should find the girl and demand she tell us what happened."

"I don't think she can do that," Madeline said softly.

Cecily gave her a sharp look. Madeline's face wore an expression Cecily knew well. "Something's happened," she said, silently praying it wasn't bad news.

Madeline's shoulders lifted in a shrug. "I don't know. At least, I'm not sure. But I think we're about to find out."

"Oh, for heaven's sake, Madeline—" Phoebe began, but she was interrupted by a sharp tap on the door.

With a familiar sense of impending doom, Cecily watched Baxter walk into the room.

"I apologize for interrupting your meeting, madam, but I have some rather grave news," he said after acknowledging each of the women with a slight bow.

"Have they found Ivy Glumm?" Phoebe asked, her eyes opening wide as she leaned forward.

Baxter kept his gaze firmly on Cecily's face and raised his eyebrow a fraction.

Interpreting his unspoken question, Cecily sighed. Obviously it was bad news. There didn't seem any point in trying to conceal it, however. Bad news traveled with lightning speed in the Pennyfoot. "You can tell me what it is, Baxter. I'm sure the ladies will be discreet."

"Naturally," Madeline murmured, while Phoebe nodded her head so hard that the huge brim of her hat flapped up and down like a giant tiddlywink caught in a slow spin.

"Very well, madam." Baxter stretched his neck above the stiff white collar, a gesture that told Cecily he was more than a little disturbed. "Ivy Glumm has been found in the woods near Deep Willow Pond. I regret to tell you that the inspector is on his way and wishes to question everybody concerned."

"Oh, my," Phoebe whispered. "I suppose that will include me."

Cecily barely heard her. "Is she . . . ?" She left the question unfinished, but Baxter nodded, sympathy brimming in his gray eyes. "Yes, madam. I'm afraid the police believe she was murdered."

Phoebe gave a little squeak, while Madeline muttered something under her breath.

"And the last place she was seen alive was here at the Pennyfoot," Cecily said slowly.

"Precisely." Baxter cleared his throat. "I'm sorry, madam."

Once more it seemed that the hotel was threatened. She looked up at him, drawing strength from his presence. "So am I, Baxter," she muttered. "So am I."

CHAPTER

🏵 4 🏵

After Baxter's stark announcement, Cecily had little enthusiasm left for discussion of the preparations for the tea dance. Apparently sensing her need to be alone with her manager, Madeline left, coercing a reluctant and inquisitive Phoebe to leave with her.

Baxter waited for the door to close behind them, then abruptly dropped his formality and strode down the length of the table to close his arm around Cecily's shoulders. "Cecily, my dear, try not to overly concern yourself. I'm sure this can all be straightened out."

Cecily raised a hand to cling to his. How comforting it was to have someone to reassure her again. She had been alone for so long after James, her late husband, had died. Baxter had always been a stalwart friend and protector, but only recently had their relationship advanced to a personal level. She had forgotten how essential was an emotional bond in order to achieve true happiness.

She felt that joy in her heart now, and her only regret was the necessity to keep that side of their relationship a secret. She had to agree with Baxter, however, that it was best for the smooth operation of the hotel if they maintained a professional attitude in front of the staff.

She smiled up at him now, reassured by his words. "Yes, of course. After all, the hotel can hardly be held responsible for the poor girl's death, since it didn't happen here on the premises."

She saw his expression change and knew at once there was something he hadn't told her. She waited, her apprehension growing, as he took hold of her hand in both of his.

"Cecily, Ivy Glumm was buried in the woods. From what I understand from the colonel, who I must admit was somewhat incoherent, the constabulary believe she died somewhere else and was later brought to the woods to be buried. Which is why the inspector is anxious to question everyone."

"He suspects she was killed here in the hotel?"

Baxter looked unhappy. "I imagine the possibility has crossed his mind."

"How did she die?"

"Fortescue didn't know. He left the station before the body was brought back there."

She felt a cold draft across her back, as if someone had opened a window. "How did the colonel know about this?"

"He discovered her body while on his way to the George and Dragon. He arrived back here a few minutes ago."

"Oh, Lord. He must be in a terrible state. I'm surprised he was able to tell you anything."

"He was a little difficult to understand at first, I must admit. I accompanied him to the bar, however, where a large brandy helped to restore his composure." Baxter shook his head. "What little he possesses, in any case."

"Where is he now?"

"In the drawing room. He ordered another brandy, and I left him to finish it."

Cecily withdrew her hand and gathered up her notes. "I'd like to speak to him before the inspector gets here. I want to be sure the colonel doesn't say anything incriminating. You know how confused the man gets, especially after a glass or two of brandy."

"Is that wise? You know how Inspector Cranshaw despises your interference in police business."

"I know how desperately the inspector would like to close down the Pennyfoot." She rose to her feet as Baxter pulled back her chair. "As you well know, while he suspects the presence of our gaming rooms in the cellars, his hands are tied, since he cannot afford to offend the aristocracy by investigating the premises. The only way he can put an end to the gambling is to find an excuse to close us down. Any excuse."

Baxter smoothed a hand over his graying hair. "I am aware of that. I don't feel that we can rely on Fortescue to defend us, however, and you could even make matters worse."

"That's a risk I shall have to take. I need to know what the police know if I'm to deal with Inspector Cranshaw."

"If you can get any sense out of the old fool."

Cecily smiled up at him. "Smooth out that frown, Baxter dear. I know how to handle the colonel."

"I'm not sure anyone knows how to handle that gentleman." He reached for her hand again and lifted it to his lips. "I'd like to accompany you, but I have an appointment to interview a new gardener in a few minutes."

"Ah, yes." Cecily moved away from him and hurried to the door. "I do hope he proves satisfactory. I never realized how difficult it would be to find a competent gardener. I'm afraid I took poor John for granted. I doubt if we shall ever be able to replace him."

"We'll find someone sooner or later," Baxter promised as he followed her out into the hallway. "I have high hopes for this candidate. At least he's had some experience.''

''I don't suppose you've heard when the new telephone will be installed?'' Cecily asked hopefully.

Baxter shook his head. ''I was warned about the long delay when I ordered it.''

''Seven months ago. I do trust they haven't forgotten us entirely?''

''I remind the telephone company on a regular basis,'' Baxter assured her as they walked down the hall together. ''I'm told it could be any day now. At least we have priority, being a business. Can you imagine how long the wait would be if we were simply a residence?''

There were times, Cecily thought, when she would dearly love to be sharing a house with Baxter, instead of a busy seaside hotel. In spite of the Pennyfoot's success, due largely to the members of the aristocracy, the massive debts incurred by the remodeling of the ancient mansion seemed insurmountable at times. When something like this happened, her worries were intensified.

If it weren't for turning a blind eye to the dubious pursuits of London's upper crust, Cecily might well have lost the Pennyfoot after James died. As it was, she provided a means for gentlemen of breeding to enjoy a respite from the hustle and bustle of city life.

Secure in the isolation of the tiny village, they could gamble or entertain a lady friend without fear of notoriety. Rumors abounded that King Edward himself had taken advantage of the discreet amenities available at the hotel. So far no one had actually proved that, and Cecily refused to discuss the subject. Hurrying toward the drawing room, she hoped that the colonel would still be in control of his senses. Conversation with the elderly gentleman was unpredictable at the best of times.

She found him seated in a deep armchair by the fireplace, nodding over a half-filled glass of brandy. Fortunately he was alone, the rest of the guests no doubt taking advantage of the fine spring weather.

"Ah, there you are, old bean!" he bellowed when she spoke his name. "Come to join me in a spot of the old mother's ruin, what?"

His words were only slightly slurred, and Cecily quickly took a seat opposite him before he attempted to get to his feet. "Not at the moment, Colonel. Actually I wanted to ask you about the discovery of Ivy Glumm. Can you tell me exactly how you managed to find her?"

Fortescue frowned. "Ivy what? Not sure I know the lady. Friend of yours, is she?"

Cecily shook her head. "Desiree," she said gently. "The Great Denmarric's assistant."

The colonel's eyes began blinking rapidly up and down, a sure sign that he was agitated. "Oh, that. Yes, well, wasn't me who found her, old bean. It was the dog. Big brute, it was. Bore the mark of the Lord on its head, poor blighter. Howling like a blasted banshee."

"Oh, dear," Cecily murmured.

Tilting his glass to his lips, he swallowed a mouthful of brandy. "Had to go and see what all the fuss was about, what? That's when I saw the hand sticking out of the ground. Took a look, saw the sequins, knew right away where I'd seen her before."

"Did you happen to see anyone else in the area?" Cecily asked, not too hopefully.

The colonel shuddered. "Not a soul, old bean. Only the dog. Reminds me of the time I was in India. Sergeant Major was a big chap, voice like a blasted foghorn. Anyway—"

"Can you tell me what the dog looked like?"

He blinked at her and hiccupped. "How'd you know about the dog?"

"You told me, Colonel," Cecily answered with what she considered quite remarkable patience.

He hiccuped again and gave his mouth a light pat. "I did? Well, I'll be blowed. I don't remember that. I was just starting to tell you about the Sergeant Major. He—"

"Colonel!" Cecily softened her sharp tone with a smile. "The dog?"

Fortescue looked confused. "Well, yes, old bean, I was just coming to that. Sergeant Major had a dog, you see. Massive beast, with a bark that could split your head in half."

Cecily sighed. "I was talking about the dog you saw this morning."

"Anyway, when he lined up the troops for inspection, the dog would sit a few yards away and bark every time the sergeant major issued an order. Sounded just like the ruddy bloke, too. Then one night the dashed dog barked at a rat or something—at two o'clock in the morning. Half the blasted barracks turned out on parade before they realized it wasn't the sergeant major barking orders. Dog disappeared after that. I heard—"

"Colonel, would you care for another brandy?" Cecily offered desperately.

Fortescue blinked at her. "Oh, say, old girl, don't mind if I do. Jolly decent of you, and all that."

"I'll have one sent in to you when I leave. But first I'd like to hear about the dog you saw this morning." She waited while the colonel appeared to be struggling with his elusive memory. It was amazing how Fortescue could remember so much about his days in the military yet had trouble remembering what had happened to him just hours ago.

"Big black brute," he finally muttered, staring into his glass.

Cecily decided to give up on the dog for the moment. "Did you notice any injuries to the body?"

The colonel shuddered. "Didn't look, old girl. Took one look at the sequins and rushed down to the pub. Next thing I know, the constable has me down at the station. Sent me back here in a carriage. Dashed decent of him, what?"

"Very," Cecily agreed. She wondered if P.C. Northcott had managed to get any more information out of the colonel

than she had. All she could do now was to wait for the
inspector to arrive. Promising the colonel she'd have his
brandy sent in right away, she left him muttering into his
glass something about dogs.

Mrs. Chubb had been the housekeeper at the Pennyfoot
Hotel ever since it had opened. She'd seen a good many
changes take place, the most noticeable of which, as far as
she was concerned, being the installation of the indoor lavatory.

Although the staff were not permitted to use the conven-
ience, they did, of course, clean it, and for weeks the topic
of conversation amongst the housemaids was the miracle
of a commode that emptied itself.

Even that had paled into significance, however, with the
news that the Pennyfoot was to have a telephone installed.
For many months, the event had been the subject of excited
speculation in the kitchen.

Having been informed that the phenomenon was now
imminent, Mrs. Chubb began to worry about the consequences of instant communication. She was worried that
the maids would spend all day talking to their boyfriends
instead of getting on with their work. With that in mind,
she decided to make her announcement and follow it with
some dire warnings.

She waited until after lunch, when Gertie, Ethel, and
Doris were all in the kitchen together. Michel, the Pennyfoot's renowned chef, was also there, which Mrs. Chubb
could have done without. Michel had a nasty habit of butt-
ing into things that didn't concern him.

Walking into the steam-filled kitchen, Mrs. Chubb
clapped her hands to attract the maids' attention. Doris,
who was shoveling coal into the hungry mouth of the oven,
turned around immediately.

Gertie and Ethel were deep in a private conversation as
usual and completely ignored the housekeeper's command.

Michel threw a disdainful glance in her direction and promptly turned his back on her.

"Ethel! Gertie! Will you kindly pay attention to what I have to say?" Mrs. Chubb demanded. "It's no wonder you girls can't get your work done when you spend half the day prattling like that."

"I'd like the bleeding chance to talk for bloody half a day," Gertie muttered. "I've only just opened me blinking mouth, and you're bleeding starting on me."

Mrs. Chubb rolled her eyes to the ceiling. She had long ago given up on curing Gertie of her foul mouth, but hearing her swear like that never ceased to irritate her. "I have something of importance to tell you," she said, glaring at Gertie to indicate her disapproval, "and I want you to listen carefully. I have just heard the telephone will soon be installed in the main lobby of the hotel."

Her next words were drowned out by a chorus of excited exclamations. Even Michel had turned back to listen to her, though he did his best to look as if he wasn't interested.

Pleased with the effect of her announcement, Mrs. Chubb folded her chubby arms across her ample breast. "Obviously, the telephone will be for the use of the guests, as well as madam and Mr. Baxter. I have been informed, however, that anyone on the staff may have the use of the telephone if it is an emergency."

"Blimey," Gertie said, giving Ethel a hearty nudge with her elbow. "You'll be able to talk to the George and Dragon and find out if your bleeding hubby's down there boozing it up."

"My Joe doesn't have time to go to the pub," Ethel said with a toss of her head. "And he's not a boozer, neither." Her last words ended on a fit of coughing, and it took her a moment or two to get her breath.

Gertie shook her head in disgust. "All right, keep your bleeding hair on. I was only flipping joking."

Mrs. Chubb seized the opportunity to press home her point. "No one on this staff will be talking to anyone unless it's a matter of life and death. I hope I make myself clear?''

"What I don't understand," Doris muttered as she heaved more coal into the smoldering oven, "is how your voice can get all the way to London just by talking into a thing on the wall."

"Transmission," Michel said, his thick French accent holding a note of superiority.

Gertie emitted a most unladylike whistle. " 'Ere, 'ark at him, for Gawd's sake. Where'd you come up with a bleeding word like that?''

"Gertie, for heaven's sake," Mrs. Chubb snapped. "Kindly refrain from making those disgusting noises."

"What, this?" Gertie pursed her lips and let out an even louder whistle.

Doris giggled while Ethel looked up at the ceiling.

Mrs. Chubb summoned her most forbidding glare. "If you know what's good for you, my girl, you won't let me hear that again."

"Why not?" Gertie demanded. "I hear Michel bleeding whistling all the bloody time. What's wrong with me doing it, too?''

"It's not ladylike. And it's certainly not considered proper for a young lady to whistle like some guttersnipe in a back alley."

Gertie turned to Ethel with a look of outrage on her face. "See what I bleeding mean? It's all right for a bleeding bloke to whistle, but it ain't proper for a blinking lady. I tell you, Ethel, when I come back next time, it'll be as a bleeding man."

"*Sacre bleu,*" Michel muttered, hitting his forehead with the heel of his hand. "Tell me the world will not have to suffer Gertie in a man's body."

"Oo, 'eck," Ethel said, solemnly staring at Gertie, "you'd have to wear trousers and everything. And cut your hair."

Gertie tucked a thick strand of her jet black hair under her cap. "I tell you bleeding what, it would be flipping easier to take care of, that's what I bloody say.''

Aware that she was losing control of the situation, Mrs. Chubb slammed her hands together again. Doris jumped, dropping lumps of coal onto the hearth. "Please pay attention. I want you to understand that you will only use the telephone with special permission from me or Mr. Baxter. Under no circumstances will you be permitted to ring everyone in Badgers End, willy-nilly, just to have a chat.''

Michel let out an explosive and clearly derisive laugh. "You cannot talk to everyone in Badgers End on the telephone, Mrs. Chubb. It is eempossible.''

"I fail to see the humor in that," Mrs. Chubb said stiffly. "I'm trying to impress upon these girls that the telephone is not a plaything. I'd appreciate it if you would mind your own business, Michel.''

The chef carefully put down the heavy frying pan he was holding. Straightening his tall chef's hat, he lifted his chin and gave Mrs. Chubb one of his haughty looks down his nose. "It is obvious you not understand how ze telephone works. You cannot talk to someone else, unless zey too have ze telephone. I doubt if there is more than one dozen telephones in the entire village. I make sense, *oui?*''

Mrs. Chubb was not to be outdone. Huffing out her breath, she stared Michel straight in the eye. "Let me tell you, Michel, I know these girls. Mark my words, they'd find a way.''

The door opened behind her then, much to her relief. She was on flimsy ground as far as the telephone was concerned. She didn't understand how it worked, nor did she care to. She'd managed all her life without it, and she couldn't see what all the excitement was about. Nasty, new-fangled things popping up all over the place—whatever was the world coming to?

"Guess what I just heard," Samuel's voice said behind her.

"We're going to get a bleeding telephone in the lobby," Gertie said with a smug look on her face. "And you're not going to be bloody allowed to use it, so there.''

"It's not about the telephone," Samuel said breathlessly. "It's much more exciting than that."

Mrs. Chubb turned to look at him. She didn't care for the look on his face. If she didn't know Samuel better, she'd say he was scared about something. Even Gertie fell silent, waiting for Samuel to deliver his news.

He walked into the center of the kitchen and looked around at them all. "They found Ivy Glumm," he announced, looking at each of them in turn.

Mrs. Chubb was well used to Samuel's theatrics, but even she felt a chill brush her spine. "Is she all right?" she asked sharply.

"No, she ain't." Samuel pulled the cap off his head and twisted it around in his hands. "She's dead, that's what." He lowered his voice to a hoarse, menacing whisper. "The bobbies think she was buried alive."

CHAPTER

❄ 5 ❄

Inspector Cranshaw arrived that afternoon, a tall gaunt man with a sour expression and a terse manner intended to intimidate. Cecily had always managed to hold her own, however, and she greeted him with her customary smile, which he chose not to return.

He stood in the library, P.C. Northcott hovering at his elbow, and gazed at the rows of books as if he'd never seen them before. "I trust that the ballroom has been kept off-limits to the guests since last night?"

Sensing the hint of a threat behind the question, Cecily hastened to reassure him. "The area of the stage has been roped off, Inspector. As you are aware, the ballroom also serves as the dining room at mealtimes."

Cranshaw flicked a glance in her direction. "Nevertheless, I intend to have the entire room under guard. You will be permitted to use the dining area, but my men will be posted there to ensure that no one disturbs the area of the stage. There will be a twenty-four-hour watch in the ballroom until this murder is solved.''

Cecily tightened her mouth. In her opinion such a stringent procedure was unnecessary. It was bound to make things uncomfortable during mealtimes. It was particularly frustrating since the inspector had no proof whatsoever that the murder had been committed on the premises.

She knew better than to argue with him at this stage, however. ''As you wish,'' she said demurely. ''I'll inform my staff of the arrangement.''

''I would also like to emphasize at this point that if anyone, and I mean anyone, approaches the stage area, they will be instantly detained.''

Cecily pursed her lips. She knew quite well that Cranshaw's warning was aimed directly at her. ''I understand, Inspector. I'll take care to make my staff aware of your instructions.''

''I am much obliged.''

He turned to leave, and she said quickly, ''Inspector, may I ask how Ivy Glumm died?''

Without even glancing at her, he said stiffly, ''That has not been ascertained as yet. Good day, Mrs. Sinclair.''

Even if he did know the answer to her question, Cecily doubted he would have told her. She would have to obtain that information elsewhere.

''Entire room under guard,'' P.C. Northcott muttered as he laboriously copied down the inspector's orders in his tattered notebook. ''Permitted to—''

''Come along, Constable,'' Cranshaw barked as he headed for the door.

''Yes, sir, of course, sir,'' Northcott mumbled, still scribbling in his notebook as he followed his superior out into the hallway.

Cecily waited until they were out of earshot before letting out an explosive sigh. Knowing how long it would take the inspector to investigate a case like this, it would seem that the tea dance was in jeopardy. A number of prominent guests would be disappointed.

Several ladies were also planning to attend the presentations of the new fashions, an event that Cecily had arranged several weeks ago and which was supposed to take place immediately after the tea dance. Since the event was the sole purpose of their visit to the hotel, Cecily concluded, she would either have to inform the ladies that the event was canceled or . . .

Her gaze went involuntarily to the space over the fireplace where her late husband's portrait used to hang. She had wanted to place a portrait of Baxter there, but he had declined the offer, saying he had no wish to supersede his old friend. Instead, Cecily had a large seascape hung there, until she could decide what she wanted for a permanent replacement.

Cecily rather missed James's portrait. She had sorted out many of her chaotic thoughts by talking aloud to the image of her dead husband. Attempting to converse with a painting of a vast, raging ocean just wasn't the same.

But now she had Baxter, she reminded herself. He was the one she should be talking to. If only she could be sure he would understand her dilemma. She had made a promise to inform him of her intentions if they involved any hint of danger. In return he had promised to hold his silence in order to protect the hotel and its staff. This would be the first time that promise would be tested.

Knowing Baxter as she did, he would not find it easy to agree to her wishes. But the only alternative she could see to canceling the events that were so important to the financial stability of the hotel was to investigate the murder herself.

Anticipating trouble with Baxter over that, she headed for the kitchen to inform the staff of the police guard in the ballroom.

•　•　•

"Buried alive?" Gertie repeated, staring at Samuel. "Who'd do a thing like that to Ivy Glumm?"

"Not who . . ." Samuel looked around him as if expecting someone to jump out from somewhere. "What."

"What?"

Samuel nodded. "That's what I said. What."

Gertie rolled her eyes. "No, you bleeding twerp, I mean what do you mean? What flipping what?"

Mrs. Chubb clicked her tongue. "Stop this nonsense right now. Samuel, either tell us what you mean or get back to the stables and let these girls get on with their work."

Samuel lifted his hands in mock surrender. "I'm trying to, Mrs. Chubb. All I'm saying is how Ivy disappeared while she was in the box. Nobody saw her leave, yet when Denmarric opened the door, she was gone. I reckon it were evil spirits what got her."

"Spirits?" Doris echoed with a squeak, while Ethel clutched her throat and muttered, "Oh, my."

Over by the stove, Michel crashed a saucepan lid onto the stove. No one took any notice of him. They were all staring at Samuel.

"There are no such things as evil spirits," Mrs. Chubb declared.

"Madeline Pengrath bleeding thinks there is," Gertie said, feeling a cold shiver around her neck.

"What's worse," Samuel went on, obviously enjoying all the attention he was getting, "they're still here."

"W-who's still here?" Doris asked, wringing her hands together.

Samuel looked at her and bared his teeth in a ghastly grin. "The evil spirits, that's who. Trapped inside them boxes what the magician had to leave behind on the stage. That's why they're putting bobbies on guard in the ballroom, so's no one will go up there and let the spirits out. 'Cos if you do, they'll whisk you all away and bury you alive in the woods on Putney Downs."

"*Sacre bleu,*" Michel muttered and crossed himself.

Doris moaned in fright and grabbed hold of Ethel's arm.

"Oo 'eck," Ethel whispered.

"For bleeding sake, Samuel, stop flipping frightening everybody," Gertie snapped, unwilling to admit she was as scared as the rest of them. "You're bloody well making all this up."

"No I'm not," Samuel said, holding his hand over his heart. "I swear I'm not."

"Samuel, if you're deliberately frightening my girls—" Mrs. Chubb began, but before she could finish the sentence, the door opened and madam walked in.

Gertie and the two maids bobbed a curtsey, while Samuel respectfully bowed his head. Mrs. Chubb sounded flustered as she greeted the new arrival.

"What can I do for you, mum? Is there something I can get for you? A nice cup of tea?"

Madam shook her head, her face quite serious. "Thank you, Mrs. Chubb, but I came by to give you some very bad news, I'm afraid."

Mrs. Chubb nodded. "We heard, mum. They found Ivy, poor child."

Madam raised her eyebrows. "Who told you?"

"I did," Samuel said. "I was in the George and Dragon when Colonel Daffy . . . I mean Fortescue . . . came in babbling about what he'd seen up in the woods."

"I see." Madam gave Samuel a sharp look. "Anyway, I'm afraid Inspector Cranshaw has posted a guard over the entire ballroom, including the dining area, until the murder is solved."

"See?" Samuel said triumphantly. "I told you I wasn't lying."

Doris moaned again, while Mrs. Chubb shook her head and clucked her tongue.

Gertie felt an ominous churning in her stomach. "Then there were really bleeding evil spirits what buried Ivy alive?"

Madam looked startled. "Buried alive?"

"That's what Samuel flipping said."

"That's what I heard," Samuel said stoutly.

"Perhaps I could have a word with you later, Samuel," madam said, giving him another sharp look. "I'll see you an hour from now in the library."

"Yes, mum." Samuel touched his forehead with his fingers.

"I'd appreciate it if you would all keep this to yourselves," madam said, looking around at everybody. "I don't want the guests disturbed any more than necessary."

Gertie joined in the chorus of "Yes, mum!" She waited until madam had left, then said defiantly, "I ain't going to let no bleeding spirits frighten me, so there. As long as they're locked up in the bloody boxes, they can't hurt us. Ain't that right, Mrs. Chubb?"

Mrs. Chubb nodded briskly, though Gertie could tell she wasn't all that sure. "Of course. Now let's forget this nonsense and get on with the work, or we'll never be ready for afternoon tea. When I come back, I want to see all the tea trays set up on the tables and the sandwiches cut. Is that clear?"

Without waiting for an answer, she whirled around and flew out the door.

Gertie picked up the stack of silver trays from the sideboard. "Well, I might as well go and start laying the tables," she announced, trying to sound offhand: "It's your turn to do the teapots, Ethel. Doris, you can bring the cutlery, and we'll all go in there together."

"Perhaps we will have ze good luck and you will all get carried off by ze evil spirits," Michel said, brandishing a wooden spoon like a sword.

"Perhaps we'll be lucky, and you'll drop bleeding dead," Gertie muttered as she led the way out of the kitchen.

"Perhaps we'll be lucky and find a handsome policeman waiting for us in the dining room," Ethel said hopefully.

" 'Ere, watcha talking about, Ethel Salter?" Gertie demanded, humping the trays onto her wide hip. "You already got a bleeding man, so keep your blinking paws off of them bobbies."

"I meant for you," Ethel said, sounding a little too innocent.

"Yeah? Well, I ain't bleeding interested, so there." Gertie puffed a little as she climbed the stairs to the lobby.

"I bet if Ross McBride came strolling around the corner, you'd be interested," Ethel said slyly.

Gertie felt her stomach rise up and plop down again at the sound of the Scotsman's name. "He's not bleeding likely to, is he, seeing as how he's hundreds of miles away in flipping Scotland."

"You could talk to him on the telephone," Doris suggested.

Gertie almost dropped the trays at the thought. Just fancy, being able to hear his voice through a trumpet small enough to fit on her ear. "I wouldn't know what to say to him," she said when she'd recovered her voice.

"Tell him you sleep with his letters under your pillow," Ethel said, grinning at Doris.

Doris giggled, and Ethel joined in, only to lose her breath again in another fit of coughing.

"I'll bleeding tell them blinking spirits to pin your mouth shut," Gertie said tartly. She didn't like talking about Ross McBride this way. Her feelings for Ross were special, and she wanted to keep them all to herself. The burly Scotsman was the only man she'd even looked at since Ian had confessed to her that their marriage wasn't proper since he was already married.

She'd been expecting the twins at the time, though she hadn't known they were twins, not until they were born. She'd vowed then that she'd never look at another man as long as she lived. But then Ross had come along, with his kind face and gentle hands, and she'd found herself thinking about him all the time.

He'd made her feel pretty and clever, not clumsy and

stupid, the way Ian had made her feel. Gertie sighed. She missed Ross. She really missed him. Much more than she ever thought she would. It would be nice to talk to him on the telephone.

Lugging the heavy trays down the hallway to the dining room, she began to rehearse what she would say to him. Just in case she ever got the chance.

"The entire ballroom?" Baxter looked aghast. "Is that really necessary?"

"The inspector thinks it is." Seated across the desk from him in his office, Cecily realized that Baxter was filling out in the face. Now that she really looked at him, she noticed the buttons on his vest were straining just a little. A sign of contentment, she thought, with a little rush of warmth.

"You don't seem too perturbed by the news," Baxter commented, giving her a shrewd look.

She quickly concentrated on the matter at hand. "Of course I'm upset. This will make things uncomfortable for the guests at mealtimes, not to mention the fact that if this murder isn't solved by the end of the week, we stand to lose a good number of our bookings if we have to cancel the tea dance and fashion presentation."

Baxter shook his head. "I can't believe that someone actually murdered Ivy Glumm right under our noses. How did he get her out of the hotel without anyone seeing him, that's what I'd like to know."

"Precisely, which makes me think that Ivy wasn't murdered in the hotel, but was perhaps abducted and killed later. There's also Samuel's statement to consider."

"Samuel? What does he have to do with it?"

"Samuel says he heard that Ivy had been buried alive."

"Good Lord!" Baxter sat up on his chair. "What a ghastly thought."

"I agree. If it's true, however, then Ivy wasn't actually killed in the hotel."

"Nevertheless, if she was abducted as you seem to think,

I doubt that the inspector will make a distinction.''

"Probably not." Cecily drew in a deep breath. "If we wait for the inspector to solve the case, however, we will lose a great deal of money. Therefore I feel compelled to investigate the murder myself.''

Baxter's brows drew together. "Absolutely not. If it's true that Ivy Glumm was abducted and buried alive, we are dealing with an extremely dangerous criminal. I would be insane to let you go poking your nose into something that could literally be the death of you.''

"Which is precisely why you must help me," Cecily said serenely.

Baxter opened his mouth for a ready retort, then shut it again with a snap. After a moment or two he muttered, "I was afraid of this. I had hoped your sleuthing days were over.''

"And I had hoped there would be no more necessity for my sleuthing, as you put it.''

"I suppose you've made up your mind about this.''

"Yes, Baxter, I'm afraid I have.''

He was silent for a long moment, then sat back in his chair with a heavy sigh. "Very well. I know from painful experience how fruitless it is to attempt to dissuade you when you have your mind set. I made you a promise, however, and I will honor it. On the condition that you do not make a move without me knowing about it.''

"You have my word." Pleased with herself, she adroitly changed the subject. "Now, tell me, how did our new gardener fare in your interview?''

"He didn't," Baxter said shortly. "When I questioned him, he couldn't tell the difference between a delphinium and a daisy. He actually thought a topiary was a summer house.''

"Oh, dear," Cecily murmured, thoroughly disappointed. "I don't know what we're going to do. The lawns badly need rolling, and the rose bushes are a shambles. I was hoping to have the renovations to the roof garden finished by now. We shall soon be into our busy season again.''

''I know.'' Baxter threw down his pencil in a gesture of disgust. ''It is really becoming quite difficult to find adequate staff these days. So many of our young people are moving to the city, and I can't say I blame them. With all this modern technology opening up, they can easily find well-paying jobs in the factories. No one wants to work on the land anymore.''

''Or in service,'' Cecily said with a sigh. ''Somehow I have the feeling that one day most of us will have to do without servants.''

''The world is changing, Cecily. I well remember how many times you assured me that we would have to change with it.''

She smiled. ''Sometimes it's easier said than done.''

He smiled back at her. ''Well, in the midst of all this gloom and doom, I do have a small ray of sunshine. The telephone will be installed tomorrow morning.''

''Oh, my.'' She clasped her hands in delight. ''I'm really quite excited about it. Imagine being able to talk to someone in London without ever having to leave the hotel. It really is quite miraculous.''

Baxter nodded. ''Yes, well, I don't want to dampen your enthusiasm, dear madam, but it has been my experience that miracles can sometimes bring their own set of problems. Particularly the technological ones. I trust you haven't forgotten our experiences with the lavatory when it was installed?''

Cecily shuddered. ''How could I forget? It took weeks to get the smell out of the carpets.''

''Exactly. And now there is talk of bringing electricity to our part of the coast. Imagine the problems that will cause.''

Electricity. Cecily closed her eyes. The very word conjured up all kinds of possibilities. Living in today's world was a little like visiting the treasure caves of Ali Baba. One never knew quite what would be discovered next.

Unfortunately the problems of the world didn't vanish with the onset of new horizons. There were still bills to be paid and a murder to be solved. The sooner she began her investigation, the better.

CHAPTER

❈ 6 ❈

"I do wish madam would hurry up and find a gardener," Mrs. Chubb grumbled as she opened a sack of potatoes. "These vegetables are nowhere near as good as the ones John used to grow in the garden."

For once Michel agreed with her. "It is eempossible to find another gardener like John. I have tried many farms, but ze spring cabbage . . . it has no taste, and ze potatoes have ze black eyes."

Mrs. Chubb nodded. "I know what you mean. It's funny how you never really appreciate someone until after they're gone. I know there'll never be another gardener like John, but anyone would be better than having all this stuff delivered from the farms. By the time it gets here, it's all wilting. Just look at this lettuce."

"Ross knows how to do gardening," Gertie said without thinking.

Mrs. Chubb gave her a sharp look. "You're not still

writing letters to that Scotsman, are you, Gertie? You shouldn't encourage him like that. Leave him be so that he can find someone who can care for him, that's what I say.''

Gertie didn't answer but went on spreading the fish paste on the wafer-thin slices of bread. She felt guilty, remembering all the letters tucked away in her chest of drawers. Ned, the doorman, slipped them to her on the quiet, so no one would know she got two a week. She couldn't bear the thought of Mrs. Chubb nosing into her thoughts and dreams about Ross.

She hadn't even told Ethel what was in the letters—how Ross said he missed her and couldn't stop thinking about her.

Gertie smiled to herself. Ross had told her how he liked to grow things in the garden. It kept his mind off how much he wanted to see her, he'd said.

"What are you grinning at, Gertie Brown?" Mrs. Chubb's harsh voice made Gertie jump.

"I was just thinking about something Ethel said." Gertie gave Mrs. Chubb an innocent look. "She can be bloody funny sometimes."

The housekeeper shook her head, her face creased in worry lines. "I don't know how funny she can feel with that dreadful cough. I don't like the sound of it, I don't at all."

Gertie's smile vanished. "I thought it was getting bleeding better."

"Well, it was for a while." Mrs. Chubb rubbed her hands together and headed back to the pantry. "When she went to see Dr. Prestwick, he gave her something for it and it went away. But now it's back. I hear her coughing all the way down the hallway."

She disappeared into the pantry, and Gertie stared after her, her preoccupation with Ross forgotten. Now that she came to think about it, Ethel had been coughing a bit lately. Gertie had been so wrapped up in her daydreams that she just hadn't paid attention.

As soon as she saw Ethel, Gertie decided, she'd tell her to go back to the doctor's. He'd give her some more medicine. Then she'd be all right.

Thus assured, Gertie went back to spreading the fish paste. In spite of her convictions, however, somewhere in the back of her mind a little knot of worry refused to go away.

Samuel was already waiting in the library when Cecily returned there later. He stood by the fireplace, twisting his cap around and around in his fingers as he struggled to recount the colonel's garbled words.

"He kept talking about the dog," Samuel said, creasing his brow in an effort to remember. "It were the dog what led him to her. He saw her hand sticking out."

Cecily nodded. "Yes, he told me. He doesn't seem to remember much else. Did he talk about seeing anyone else out there in the woods?"

Samuel gave a definite shake of his head. "No, mum. He didn't."

"How did you discover that the police believe Ivy was buried alive?"

Samuel looked down at his feet. "Well, mum, I don't know how true it is, like, but I was talking to one of the bobbies what's on guard in the dining room, and he says as how there wasn't a mark found on Ivy's body, and they don't know what killed her. The bobby said as how it looked as if she might have been buried alive."

"I see." Cecily pursed her lips. "So you are merely jumping to conclusions, Samuel."

"Yes, mum, I suppose I was," Samuel said unhappily.

"I don't have to tell you how dangerous it is to spread rumors that have not been substantiated."

"Yes, mum. I mean . . . no, mum."

"And I really don't think it's necessary to frighten the kitchen staff with stories of evil spirits."

Samuel looked even more distressed. "No, mum, but—"

Cecily frowned. "But what, Samuel?"

"Well, mum, it's the magician, ain't it? I mean, he was the one what made Ivy disappear. He must have sent her to the woods. But he couldn't have killed her, could he, because we was all watching him. So it must have been those spirits what live in the black beyond. That's what he said . . . that they wanted to hold her in their clutches. He knows what they done to her, I reckon, if anyone does."

Cecily gazed at him thoughtfully for a moment or two. "Perhaps he does, Samuel," she murmured at last. "Perhaps I should have a word with him."

Baxter received Cecily's announcement with as much enthusiasm as a proposed visit to the dentist. He stared at her, in fact, with such horror that one would have thought she'd informed him of the immediate demise of the hotel.

"Denmarric? Surely you don't suspect him of murdering his own assistant? How could he? He was in full view of the audience, including myself, the entire time. Unless he ran the poor girl through with the sword, in which case we surely would have seen her body, Denmarric couldn't possibly have killed Ivy Glumm."

"He certainly didn't kill her with the sword, since Samuel heard that there were no sign of injuries on Ivy's body. Denmarric is a magician, however. I wouldn't discount anything without at least talking to him. In any case, if I can persuade him to tell me how the trick was performed, that might shed some light onto exactly what happened to Ivy after she was locked in the box."

"If he is responsible for her death, he's certainly not likely to confess it," Baxter said, beginning to look stubborn.

Cecily did her best to reassure him. "Denmarric won't know we suspect him. We'll go there on the pretext of offering our condolences to him and his wife on their tragic

loss, and our assurance that his property will be taken care
of while it's impounded at the Pennyfoot. That is one of
the advantages of not having a telephone. Since we cannot
ring him and express our sympathy, we have to visit.''

She frowned at Baxter. ''I wonder if people will stop
socializing once they have a telephone.''

''If I remember, Denmarric isn't exactly the sociable
sort. He threw us out of his dressing room at the Hippodrome when you attempted to question him that time.''

''That's because he mistook us for news reporters and
was put out because we weren't there to take his photo-
graph.''

''He'll be even more put out when he realizes you suspect him of murder.''

Cecily leaned over and patted his hand. ''You worry too
much, Bax. Leave it to me. I have had some experience in
this, you know.''

''That is precisely what concerns me,'' Baxter muttered
gloomily. ''I remember those experiences only too well.''

''Everything always turned out all right in the end, did
it not?''

''More from good fortune than anything else.'' He shook
his head in despair. ''I live in dread that one day your
phenomenal luck will run out.''

''As long as I have you by my side, dear Baxter, I have
nothing to worry about.'' She crossed the room to the door,
then paused to look back at him. ''I've asked Samuel to
drop off my calling card at Denmarric's house.''

''Very well, if we must go, then we must.''

She smiled at his dismal expression. ''Don't worry, Baxter. I'll be the soul of discretion, I promise you.''

He looked up at the ceiling and steepled his fingers.
''Now where have I heard those words before?''

Even Cecily had to admit to a twinge of apprehension
as she and Baxter bowled down the Esplanade in the small
carriage later that afternoon. She well remembered their last
encounter with Denmarric and how intimidating he could

be. Baxter was a comforting presence. She would not have cared to tackle the fiery magician by herself.

Seated at his side, with the wind tugging at the silk scarf securing her hat, she normally would have enjoyed the ride to Wellercombe. It was most pleasant to be out in the fresh air, enjoying the sunshine and the fresh, clean salty breeze from the ocean.

There would be little opportunity for such jaunts once the season was fully under way. Before long the sands would be crowded with summer visitors milling about, vying for seats in front of the bandstand, or the Punch and Judy show.

Already the owners of the little shops along the promenade were busy sprucing up the windows, filling every conceivable space with trinkets, postcards, and beach toys.

"I suppose we shall have to find another housemaid if Doris does well at her audition," she remarked, raising her voice as a motorcar roared past them, trailing black smoke.

"I wouldn't worry about that just yet," Baxter said, looking longingly after the noisy vehicle. "I understand it is very difficult to gain a foothold on the stage. One has to be extremely talented."

"Doris is extremely talented. After all, that nice Mr. Kern was interested in talking to her about her singing."

"Yes, well, he was an American," Baxter said as if that explained the absurdity of the situation.

"And Bella DelRay was kind enough to arrange the audition for her. Since she is quite famous on the Variety stage, I assume she is adept at recognizing talent."

Baxter sighed. "Very well, I suppose Doris might have a small chance. I, for one, would rather not see her embark upon such an unpredictable venture."

"I agree. We shall all miss her a great deal, and I shall no doubt worry about her as much as I worry about my own sons. But we cannot hold onto our staff forever, Bax. They will all move on sooner or later, I suppose."

He surprised her by taking her gloved hand in his. "You miss your sons a great deal, I know."

"Yes, I do. I miss them both very much. I also miss not being able to see my grandson and being part of his life."

"Perhaps Michael will bring them home from Africa for a visit."

She could tell he wasn't too optimistic on that point. She was relieved when they reached Denmarric's residence and could get on with the business at hand.

The magician received them in the small drawing room, explaining that his wife had taken to her bed with a headache. Cecily wondered if he'd instructed her to stay out of sight, preferring to handle his uninvited guests himself.

"Ivy's violent death must have come as a great shock to you both," Cecily murmured, as she seated herself on a rather uncomfortable straight-back chair. The room was sparsely furnished, and Baxter declined the offer of the only other chair in the room, indicating he preferred to stand.

"It was, indeed," the magician declared in his booming voice. "My wife still has not recovered. I don't know what we shall do without Desiree. It will be difficult to find another assistant."

"I understand that well. It must take a great deal of work to teach someone how to perform those wonderful tricks."

Denmarric seemed to grow several inches. "Dogs perform tricks, madam," he barked. "I perform illusions— magic, if you will."

"Of course," Cecily said hastily, catching sight of the apprehension on Baxter's face. "That's what I meant. Your feats are really quite extraordinary. It is such a shame that this unfortunate incident with Ivy occurred, and I'm quite sure it was through no fault of your own."

"Fault?" Denmarric roared. "Of course it wasn't my fault! After all, I have made dozens of assistants disappear and never lost one of them until now."

Cecily bravely kept her smile in place. "Was there, perhaps, something different about this particular feat that you hadn't tried before? How many times had Ivy actually performed in the box?''

"The act was thoroughly rehearsed, Mrs. Sinclair." The magician narrowed his black eyes, seeming to pierce Cecily's mind. "May I ask the purpose of these questions?"

Out of the corner of her eye, Cecily saw Baxter's shoulders rise. "Merely curious, Mr. Denmarric," she murmured. "After all, it isn't often one is fortunate enough to meet a real live magician, especially one as renowned as yourself."

She'd hoped the flattery would soothe the man's prickly attitude, but he continued to glare at her as he said, "I have already faced a barrage of questions from the constabulary, Mrs. Sinclair. I do not feel inclined to answer yours."

"Mr. Denmarric, since Ivy disappeared from my hotel, I feel greatly responsible, to the point where I fear I shall have no rest until I know exactly what happened to her. Perhaps if you could explain to me how the . . . illusion was performed, it might help to set my mind at rest to know that we were not at fault."

She could literally see the mask of the Great Denmarric slip into place. Drawing himself up to his full height, he flung out an arm in a familiar theatrical gesture. "Madam, if I knew what happened to the unfortunate girl, I would be only too happy to tell you. As far as I am concerned, I performed the illusion perfectly. I cannot say what happened after that. Desiree simply disappeared and failed to return."

Cecily raised her eyebrows. "Mr. Denmarric, surely you could not have forgotten that Ivy Glumm was found buried in the woods on Putney Downs? The reason she did not return was because someone apparently took her life. That hardly constitutes an illusion, magic or not. I can assure you, the body is very real."

Denmarric's face grew dark and ominous. His brows furrowed, and his eyes were mere slits that seemed to breathe fire. In a voice that would have made a lion tremble, he shouted, "I do not have to listen to this drivel, madam! I am simply a magician who performed an illusion in full view of an audience. I made my assistant disappear. I cannot be held responsible for what happens to her once she is outside the realm of my control. Now kindly leave at once, before I am forced to remove you bodily."

"That's enough, Denmarric," Baxter said, stepping forward. "You will apologize to Mrs. Sinclair for your foul temper."

Cecily caught her breath at her manager's expression. His gray eyes glittered like icicles on a frosty morning, and she knew well the grim set of that mouth.

Denmarric turned on him, one arm sweeping the air in a gesture of defiance.

Fearing a physical confrontation, Cecily grasped Baxter's hand and tugged. "We'll be leaving you now, Mr. Denmarric," she said, with as much dignity as was possible while traveling hastily across the carpet to the door with Baxter reluctantly in tow.

"You'll not uncover my secrets, Mrs. Sinclair, no matter how much you pry. They are known only to me. Don't waste your time questioning my stagehands, either. They know nothing. Only my assistant knew how the illusion was performed, and she can no longer tell anyone. The secret is mine alone and shall remain with me!"

His voice echoed behind them, long after they'd closed the door.

Once outside in the brisk sea air, Cecily let out her breath in a puff of relief. "Oh, my, that was a close call."

"Close call? I was prepared to tear the man apart limb from limb. How dare he speak to you in that manner!"

Cecily patted Baxter's arm as her heartbeat slowly returned to normal. "He is a performer, Baxter. We have to remember he's not like other people. You should know what theater people are like—you've met enough of them at the Pennyfoot."

"I shall never understand his kind. How can we allow

Doris to mingle with people like this? She will be terrified.''

Cecily managed a weak grin. ''Doris is made of sterner stuff than you give her credit for. Besides, she will have Bella DelRay for a champion, and I would hate to see anyone try to cross that lady.''

Baxter raised his eyes to the sky and straightened his bow tie with both hands. ''I am beginning to despair for the future of womankind.'' He held out his hand to assist her into the carriage.

Climbing up onto the leather seat, Cecily sank back with a sigh. ''Well, I don't seem to have achieved very much with the magician. Except to make him very angry. I am no closer to finding out anything more about poor Ivy Glumm.''

''I will refrain from reminding you that I warned you this might happen.''

''Thank you, Baxter. I appreciate that.''

He gathered up the reins and gave them a flick. ''Perhaps now you will allow the inspector to conduct the investigation.''

She smiled and turned to look at him. ''Now, Baxter, you know better than that.''

Baxter looked grim. ''Yes, my dear madam. I'm very much afraid that I do.''

CHAPTER
7

"You're looking chipper this morning," Samuel said as Doris rushed into the kitchen carrying a heavy tray of china. "What put them roses in your cheeks, then?"

Doris dumped the tray on the sink and paused to catch her breath. "You'd have roses in your cheeks, too, Samuel Rawlins, if you'd just carried a tray that heavy all the way from the dining room."

"Nah . . . there's something about your face this morning, Bright Eyes." Samuel leaned forward in his chair and rested his elbows on the kitchen table. "You can't fool me. Something's happened."

Doris turned her back on him and lifted the huge iron cauldron up to the sink. The pot weighed almost as much as she did, and her back ached with the effort to heave it high enough to get it in under the tap.

She was bursting to tell someone about her latest news,

but she wasn't at all sure Samuel was the right one. He'd probably have a pink fit when she told him.

She turned the tap full on and waited for the pot to fill up. "I wish we had a tap with hot water in it," she said, hoping to take Samuel's mind off her excitement. "I hate having to drag this pot all the way over to the stove to heat the water. Gertie says as how the London hotels have hot water what comes out of the taps."

"It can't be the telephone. It hasn't come yet," Samuel said, coming up to stand behind her. "So what's happened? You might as well tell me, 'cos I'll hear it sooner or later."

He was right, and Doris knew it. Only she would rather tell him with someone else there. Reluctantly she turned around. "I'll tell you if you carry this pot over to the stove for me."

He studied her face for a moment. "Of course, me old ducks. You only have to ask, you know." He grunted as he lifted the brimming cauldron out of the sink. "Blimey, Doris, how the 'eck do you carry this thing, anyway? You're too little to be doing all this heavy work."

"That's what I say," Doris said eagerly. "That's why I want to go to London to be a singer."

Samuel dumped the pot on the stove, slopping the water over the sides. "Well, I wouldn't say that's going to be any better. There's a lot of dangers in the Smoke. Suppose you did get a chance to be on the stage. Where would you live? You don't get paid much to start with, you know. It's only the big stars what get paid a lot of money. You can't live on the streets. You'd last about five minutes there."

"That's just it." Unable to contain her excitement any longer, Doris pulled the letter out of her pocket. "Look, this came for me today." She thrust it into Samuel's hand.

Samuel stared down at it, a look of embarrassment on his face. "No use giving it to me," he mumbled. "You know I can't read."

"Oh, sorry, Samuel, I forgot." Doris opened the letter and began reading out loud. " 'Dear Doris, this is to let you know that I have decided to give you a home, should you do well in your audition next week. You will need somewhere to live if you are to be on the stage, and my house is much too big for one person. Think about it and let me know what you decide. We can talk about it when we meet next week. Yours truly, Bella DelRay.' ''

''That's very nice of her, I think,'' a voice said from the doorway.

Doris grinned at the young girl who stood there—a mirror image of herself holding a squirming toddler on each hip. ''That's what I say, Daisy.''

She rushed over to the babies and took one of them in her arms. ''Hello, Lillian. You going ta ta's with Daisy?''

The baby shoved a chubby fist into Doris's cheek and babbled happily. Doris laughed and handed the baby back to Daisy. ''I can't believe how fast they are growing. I'm going to miss watching them grow up.''

''You don't know if you're going to live in London yet,'' Samuel said, coming back to the table to sit down. ''You've got to get past the audition first.''

''She'll do it,'' Daisy said, heaving little James higher onto her hip. ''I always knew she'd be a singer.''

''Mrs. Chubb will miss you a lot if you go,'' Samuel muttered. ''We all will.''

''Excuse *moi*,'' Michel said from out in the hall. ''I cannot cook ze meals if I cannot get into ze kitchen, *non?*''

''Oops, sorry,'' Daisy said, scooting over to let him pass. ''I just came in to see Gertie, to tell her I'm off with the babies. Where is she, anyway?''

''I'm bleeding here, ain't I?'' Gertie stomped into the kitchen and deposited a loud smacker on the top of each baby's head. ''You taking them for a walk, then?''

Daisy nodded. ''I'm just on my way out.''

''I'm leaving, too,'' Samuel said, marching over to the door. Reaching it, he looked back at Doris. ''I think you'd be stupid to give up your home here to go and live in the Smoke. Look what it done to Ethel. She coughed so hard this morning, she was spitting blood. I wouldn't want to see you get like that. That would be the end of your singing, all right.''

Everyone was quiet for a long moment after the door closed behind them; then Gertie said loudly, ''Ethel's all right. She's just got a cold, that's all. The doctor will soon fix her up.''

''Well, it's not going to stop me from going up there,'' Doris declared. She hurried back to the sink and began stacking dishes with a good deal of clatter.

''Did you tell Gertie about the letter?'' Daisy asked. Without waiting for Doris to answer, she turned to Gertie. ''Bella DelRay told Doris she could live in her house with her.''

''I know she'd let you live there, too, Daisy,'' Doris said, beginning to feel nervous again at the thought of being in London all alone. She'd been trying to talk Daisy into going with her, but her twin didn't seem very thrilled about the idea.

''You're not going to London, too, are you Daisy?'' Gertie demanded. ''Who will look after me twins if you go?''

''I don't know what to do,'' Daisy muttered. ''I don't want to leave the babies . . . I haven't made up me mind yet.''

''*Sacre bleu!*'' The roar from the oven made them all jump. Michel looked so angry, his chef's cap quivered on his head as he glared at them all. ''All thees talk about going somewhere . . . no one will go anywhere until the work is done, *n'est-ce pas?*''

Both babies let out a howl, causing Michel to slam down a saucepan lid, which only made them howl louder.

''How can I work with thees racket going on?'' he yelled above the noise.

''All right, all right, keep your bleeding hair on,'' Gertie muttered.

''I'd best be off, then,'' Daisy said hurriedly. She carried the still-howling babies out, and the wailing gradually faded away.

Doris went on stacking the dishes, her excitement evaporating like the steam from a boiling kettle. Why did everyone have to go and spoil things for her? All she ever wanted to do was be a singer on the Variety stage. Why couldn't they all understand that? Why did things always have to be so difficult?

Gertie came up behind her and muttered in her ear, "Don't be so bleeding selfish, Doris. I need Daisy more than you do. You'll have all your bloody fancy friends up there, while me and me babies will have no flipping one."

Doris didn't answer. She was too busy feeling sorry for herself. Nobody understood how she felt. Nobody in the whole wide world.

"I've decided to pay a visit to Dr. Prestwick," Cecily announced as she walked with Baxter across the lawns to the duck pond. Baxter had asked her to inspect the grounds with him, to ascertain just how much work needed to be done in order to make the area presentable at least.

Baxter looked down at her, his face creased in concern. "You are not feeling well, Cecily?"

"I'm feeling quite fit, thank you."

She watched his mouth tighten. "I see."

"Oh, don't look like that, Baxter." She laid a hand on his arm. "I'm merely going to ask him a few questions. Surely you can't object to that?"

"I can think of no logical reason, no." His chin jutted out ominously. "The man is a rake and a fool, but he is not dangerous. At least to my knowledge."

She smiled. "You could always come along with me. I would enjoy your company."

"I don't think that would be a good idea. I have a number of tasks waiting for me here. In any case, Prestwick and I seem to grate on each other like sandpaper on steel.

I wouldn't want to upset him and spoil your chances of learning something from him.''

"I do worry about you, Bax. I sincerely hope that you stay in the best of health, for if you should fall ill, you would be forced to ask for the doctor's help.''

"I'll find one in Wellercombe first,'' Baxter muttered.

Looking across the lawns at the topiaries, Cecily sighed. "Everything is looking so ragged and unkempt. If we don't find a gardener soon, I shall be forced to come out here myself and trim those poor bushes. When I think of all the work poor John put into these gardens, it breaks my heart. I'm glad he isn't here to see this.''

Baxter paused and turned to her, taking both her hands in his. "I will redouble my efforts, my dear madam. I will find a gardener for you, if I have to go to London to recruit one.''

Riding along the Esplanade in the trap later, Cecily thought about that idea. Things really were getting quite desperate as far as the grounds were concerned. Already the weeds were threatening to take over the flower beds, and the bowling lawns had to be closed down because they were far too shaggy to accommodate the smooth wooden bowls.

Perhaps they should import a gardener from the city. That would mean giving him a room at the hotel, of course, at least until he found permanent accommodation. The more she thought about the idea, the more she liked it. It would be nice to have a resident gardener.

Yes, she decided, she would have Baxter work on it just as soon as she got back from the doctor's house.

The waiting room was full when she arrived, as usual, and she had to wait almost an hour before she was ushered into the doctor's surgery.

Prestwick smiled at her when she entered his office, but with more reservation than in the early days of their acquaintance.

Ever since Baxter had returned from London to resume

his duties at the Pennyfoot, Kevin Prestwick had abandoned his flirtatious manner with her—for which she was well and truly thankful.

Although the good doctor was the darling of the ladies of Badgers End, Cecily did not share their adulation. Apart from an initial weakness in response to his effusive flattery, she had soon grown wary of his ardent attentions. She knew quite well that he was entirely indiscriminate upon whom he showered his affections.

She also was aware of Baxter's resentment of the man and had no wish to add fuel to that particular fire. Seating herself in the deep leather armchair, she assured the doctor that she was feeling quite well.

"In that case," Prestwick said, looking severe, "I have to assume you are here to ask me more questions for which I have no answers."

"I'm sure you have the answers, Kevin," Cecily said blithely. "After all, you have had ample time to examine Ivy Glumm's body."

The doctor groaned and buried his head in his hands in mock despair. "I thought as much. You know full well I am not permitted to give you any information on a murder case."

"Of course, I understand your position." Cecily folded her hands in her lap and attempted a look of pure innocence. "While you cannot give me the facts, perhaps there is no reason why you can't give me a simple yes or no, is there?"

Prestwick lowered his hands and looked at her, and the twinkle in his eye resembled the way he used to look at her, before he had given up his pursuit of her affections. "You are incorrigible, Cecily," he said softly.

"I'm simply being practical." She looked down at her hands. "Now, my question is this, and it can be answered in one word. Was Ivy Glumm buried alive?"

"Good Lord, whoever told you that?"

She shrugged in a careless manner. "I heard it from a

member of the constabulary.'' She was stretching the truth a little, but under the circumstances she felt she would be forgiven.

''Ivy Glumm was most certainly dead when she was buried. I can assure you of that.''

''Then how did she die?''

Prestwick sighed. ''She died of heart failure. Nothing more dramatic than that, as far as I can tell. There was no mark on her body whatsoever, apart from a slight bruise on her cheek that certainly would not have caused her death.''

Cecily tried not to think of the rumors of evil spirits. ''You have no idea what caused her heart to fail?''

''Not at the present. I'm still investigating the possible reasons. I think we can safely rule out natural causes, since someone went to all the trouble of burying her, instead of reporting her death to the authorities.''

''It would be safe to assume, then, that whoever buried her must have been responsible for her death. Otherwise, as you say, why go to all the trouble of hiding the body?''

Prestwick shook his head. ''That is not for me to say. All I can tell you is that Ivy Glumm's heart stopped beating. For what reason, I have not discovered at this point in time.''

''But you do expect to discover the reason?''

''I certainly intend to try. An autopsy will most likely give me a clearer picture.''

She would have to be satisfied with that, Cecily thought as she prepared to rise. ''Thank you, Kevin. I do appreciate you confiding in me. Rest assured no one shall know of our conversation.''

''Except your manager, of course.''

Stung by his derisive tone, she said tartly, ''Baxter shares my concern for the welfare of the Pennyfoot. I don't have to explain to you the heavy losses we shall incur should it become necessary to close the hotel down because of a twenty-four-hour guard over the ballroom. It is imperative that this matter be cleared up as soon as possible."

He looked back at her, his light blue eyes turning grave as he rose to his feet with her. "I wish I could help you more, Cecily. I'm afraid that's all the information I have."

She nodded, appeased by his sincerity. "Thank you, anyway, Kevin. I bid you good day."

He moved to open the door for her, and she inclined her head in thanks. Just as she was about to pass through, he said quietly, "I have one more fact that might be of some help."

She paused to look up at him, arrested by his tone.

"I don't know if it will make much difference to your investigation," Prestwick said, keeping his voice low so that the curious women seated in the waiting room could not overhear. "For what it's worth, however, Ivy Glumm was carrying a child. About four months along, in my estimation."

Now that, Cecily thought with satisfaction, was a very interesting fact indeed.

Thinking about it on the way back to the hotel, she wondered if Denmarric was responsible for Ivy's condition. Perhaps Ivy threatened to tell his wife. If so, he could well have arranged his assistant's unfortunate end in order to preserve his reputation.

Having made the acquaintance of Charlotte Watkins, Cecily was quite certain that Denmarric's wife would have wasted no time in ensuring that the general public was aware of her husband's indiscretions, in which case Denmarric's popularity among the women would be sorely diminished.

Ivy's condition certainly gave the magician a motive. Now, Cecily mused, if only she could discover the means.

On an impulse she asked her driver to make a detour to Madeline's house. It had been some time since the two of them had visited Dolly's tea shop, and Dolly might be able to add some insight into Ivy's relationship with the bombastic magician.

Madeline was delighted to see her old friend and invited her in for some of her special home-grown herb tea. She had heard the news of Ivy's tragic death and was eager to learn all the details.

Cecily decided not to tell Madeline about her suspicions. After all, none of her notions were well founded, and as she had told Samuel earlier, it didn't pay to jump to conclusions.

Instead, she decided to wait until she had talked to Dolly before she pursued the matter further. After promising to meet Madeline for afternoon tea, Cecily returned to the hotel, looking forward to discussing the latest news with Baxter.

She had to admit, she thought as she climbed the steps of the Pennyfoot, she felt a great deal more comfortable sharing her escapades with him instead of trying to hide them, as she had done so often in the past.

She wondered what he would say when he learned that Ivy was expecting a baby. It was sad to think that not only had Ivy's life been taken, but that of a child as well.

Thinking of the unborn child made her think of her grandson. How dearly she would love to see her eldest son's child. How bitterly she resented the circumstances that kept Michael on the other side of the world with his African-born wife.

Shaking herself free of her morbid thoughts, she went in search of Baxter. She needed to discuss the latest developments in Ivy's murder. She also needed to talk about hiring a gardener from London. But most of all, she needed his reassurance and the comfort of his affection, for only Baxter could help her forget her troubles and make her smile again.

CHAPTER

8

"This is for you," Baxter said as soon as Cecily entered his office. "I thought you'd like to have it right away."

She took the long, slim envelope from him, her heart jumping when she saw the foreign stamp. "It's from Michael! I was thinking about him just a few minutes ago."

She tore it open, trying not to anticipate bad news. Letters from Africa took so long to arrive, by the time she received word of any kind, it was usually too late to do anything about it.

She quickly scanned the scrawled lines, aware of Baxter's tension as he waited for her to share the news with him. "He's pleased about the partnership," she exclaimed, unable to keep the surprise out of her voice. Michael had always mistrusted her relationship with Baxter. He'd worried that her manager might take advantage of her, which was ludicrous, of course.

"I'm happy to hear that." Baxter cleared his throat. "Does he mention your grandson?"

"Yes, he does." She caught her breath. "They've named him James after his grandfather, and Jacob after Simani's father."

"James Jacob Sinclair. It sounds very distinguished."

"Oh, my." Cecily read the line again, just to make sure she hadn't misunderstood. "They want me to visit them in Africa. Simani is anxious for me to see the baby." Unexpected tears sprang from nowhere, and she blinked.

"That's wonderful."

She smiled at him, handing him the letter to see for himself. "It is certainly unexpected. As you know, Simani and I were not on the best of terms while she was here. I'm happy that she seems to have forgiven me for my reservations about her marriage to Michael."

"I'm happy for you, too."

"Then why are you frowning?"

His smile didn't quite chase the worry lines away. "I was just thinking that now your differences with your daughter-in-law seem to be resolved, you might enjoy being with your family so much that you could very well decide to stay in Africa."

She raised her eyebrows in astonishment. "Now why would I do that?"

"You are familiar with the country, having spent time there with James while he was in the military. You have also on more than one occasion bemoaned the fact that your only grandchild lives on the other side of the world, not to mention both your sons."

She smiled fondly at him. "Much as I would dearly love to live close to Michael and Andrew, you wouldn't be there, dear Baxter. What's more, I know you could never be happy there. Nor I, for that matter. England is my home, and I have no wish to leave it. Or you. Especially you."

This time his smile swept over his entire face. "I'm delighted to hear it. Now tell me, what did you find out from Prestwick the Charmer?''

Accepting his change of subject, she related her conversation with the doctor as best as she could remember it. When she came to the part about Ivy carrying a child, Baxter looked shocked.

''Does Prestwick know who the father is?''

''Not as yet. He doesn't even know how she died, except that her heart stopped beating. So far he hasn't discovered the reason for that.''

''Perhaps Ivy took her own life, unable to face the shame of her condition.''

''And buried herself?''

Baxter shrugged. ''Someone might have come upon the body and decided to bury her.''

''Why would someone do that?''

''Perhaps afraid he would be accused of killing her?''

''Then how did she kill herself? There were no marks on the body. Nothing to suggest a violent act. Her heart simply stopped beating.''

''Strange,'' Baxter murmured, in such an odd way Cecily felt a cold shiver down her back.

''I did wonder if Denmarric might be responsible for her condition,'' Cecily said delicately. ''After all, he had ample opportunity.''

''Which could give him a reason to kill her, I suppose.'' Baxter shook his head. ''I still say it was impossible for the man to do so while in full view of the audience. Unless he trapped her somewhere and waited until later to come back to dispose of her.''

Cecily shook her head. ''I considered that. But no one saw anyone leave the stage except Denmarric, his wife, and the stage hands. Ivy certainly wasn't among them. There has been a twenty-four hour watch over the stage since then. When would Denmarric have been able to sneak back, kill Ivy, and remove her body?''

''I don't know,'' Baxter confessed. ''But I have the distinct feeling that you intend to find out. I only hope your investigations will not lead us into more hot water.''

Phoebe puffed a little as she hurried up the steps of the Pennyfoot. She was anxious to know if any progress had been made in the murder investigation. All the arrangements had been made for the tea dance, as well as the fashions presentation, and she was determined that nothing was going to prevent her from carrying out her carefully laid plans.

Ned, the doorman, greeted her with his customary uncouth remarks as she stepped into the shadowy foyer. ''Morning, Mrs. C.H. Nice titfer, that. Are them real birds sitting on it, then?''

Assuming he was referring to her hat, Phoebe lifted her chin. ''Of course they are not real, young man. What on earth would I be doing with real birds on my hat?''

Ned gave her a saucy grin. ''Waiting for the eggs to hatch, I reckon.''

Phoebe made a sound of disgust in her throat and swept past him, directly into the path of Colonel Fortescue, who had just emerged from the hallway.

Ever since that shameful episode in the rose garden when she had inadvertently consumed a measure of straight gin, she had done her utmost to avoid the colonel. She only vaguely remembered the details of that encounter, most of which were mercifully shrouded in her alcohol-induced haze, but she well remembered Algie's hysterical outburst when she had arrived home later.

Her son had practically disowned her, decrying her shameful behavior, accusing her of heaven knows what, and reminding her of her duty as the mother of the vicar to uphold the morals of his calling.

She had paid dearly for her mistake, not only with the embarrassment but also with a headache that had taken days to subside. She was not about to make another mistake like that one.

To this day she wasn't certain just how she'd indulged in such a wicked escapade. She suspected that the colonel had taken advantage of her innocence and somehow led her down the path of iniquity without her realizing it. She was bound and determined that he should not have another opportunity to mislead her in that manner.

Seeing him now, charging straight at her, she had the sinking feeling that this time she would not be so lucky in evading him.

"There you are, old girl," Colonel Fortescue bellowed as he rapidly approached at a bumbling run. "By George, it's good to see you again."

Phoebe bitterly resented being referred to as "old girl." Nevertheless, since the colonel addressed everyone that way, she didn't see the point in making her objections known. It would be a complete waste of time, in any case. The colonel would simply forget the next time he saw her.

"Good afternoon, Colonel," she said stiffly. She prayed he had forgotten about their little interlude in the rose garden. If he mentioned it now, in front of that dreadful doorman, she'd simply die.

"Just wanted to tell you, old bean," the colonel boomed as he halted in front of her, "dashed good entertainment the other night, what? That magician chappie really knows his stuff. Stroke of genius on your part, madam, bringing someone like that into the jolly old Pennyfoot, what? What?"

It wasn't often a gentleman complimented Phoebe on her organizational efforts. In spite of herself, she couldn't help preening just a little. "Well, thank you, Colonel," she gushed, lowering her eyes modestly just in case she should appear too conceited. One should accept praise gracefully, after all.

"Yes, well, as I've always said, if ever one needs some titillating excitement, Mrs. Carter-Holmes can always be guaranteed to provide it, by Jove."

Phoebe lifted her chin smartly. She had the uncomfortable feeling that he was alluding to that unfortunate incident in the rose garden. "I beg your pardon?"

"Not at all, old girl, not at all. Happy to oblige. Couldn't have done better myself, what?"

Phoebe eyed him suspiciously.

The colonel seemed oblivious of her resentment, however, and carried on blithely. "I say, too bad about that young filly popping off like that, what? Dashed bad luck, that's what I say."

Phoebe blinked. "I'm sorry, Colonel, I haven't the faintest idea what you mean."

"The magician, old girl. Or his assistant, rather. What's her name . . . Deirdre . . . Delilah . . . something like that."

"Desiree," Phoebe said, deciding that it was time to end this rather one-sided conversation. Edging around him, she added, "I agree, it was a tragedy."

"Could have knocked me down with a puff of wind when I saw her hand sticking out of the ground like that. By Jove, that gave me a nasty turn, I can tell you. What with the blasted dog howling—"

Phoebe came to an abrupt halt. "You found Ivy Glumm?"

"I did indeed, madam." Fortescue puffed out his chest. "Knew she was dead, of course. Seen many a dead body while I was out in India. Why, I remember once—"

Phoebe hastened to intervene, only too aware of how gruesome the colonel could be when recounting his adventures in the tropics. "Colonel, I'm sure that is all very interesting, but what I would really like to know is how Ivy Glumm died. I've heard rumors, of course, but nothing that makes sense. Mostly a lot of talk about evil spirits, or some such nonsense."

The colonel looked startled, and his eyelids began flapping up and down at quite an alarming rate. "Evil spirits?" he muttered hoarsely. "By Jove, madam, keep your voice down. We don't want to upset the little blighters, what?"

Startled, Phoebe looked around the foyer. "Little who, Colonel?"

The colonel dipped his head, sending a blast of gin-laced fumes into her face. "Evil spirits, madam. Ghastly creatures. Do horrible things to you if you upset them. Saw them in India once . . . crawling around in some poor chap's head—"

Thoroughly unnerved, Phoebe began backing away. At that precise moment a dreadful jangling noise echoed throughout the foyer, shattering the last of her composure. She shrieked, and the colonel leapt into the air with a howl.

"Never fear, madam, I'll protect you." He started sweeping at the air with his cane, narrowly missing the glass face of the grandfather clock.

Dimly, through her rising hysteria, Phoebe saw Baxter charge into the foyer.

"What the blazes—?"

"Spirits, man!" the colonel roared. "Can't you hear the blasted blighters? If only I could see the bastards—"

Peeking through her fingers, Phoebe saw Baxter rush over to a strange black contraption on the wall and break part of it off. The dreadful noise ceased immediately.

Phoebe was torn between having one of her turns or staying awake to see what happened next.

"Great Scott, man, that did the trick, what?" Colonel Fortescue beamed at Baxter, who inexplicably stuck the broken instrument in his ear and began talking to himself.

Phoebe decided she was having a nightmare. A moment or two later everything was explained, however, when she realized that Baxter was actually talking into one of those newfangled telephones.

She grasped the opportunity to escape when Baxter started to explain the intricacies of the instrument to the bewildered colonel. She was anxious to know why Cecily wanted to clutter up an exclusive hotel like the Pennyfoot with such a vulgar contraption.

• • •

Cecily arrived at Dolly's tea shop promptly at four. As usual, she had to wait another ten minutes for Madeline to arrive.

The tall, willowy woman hurried into the crowded tea-room, her long dark hair flying over her shoulders, her simple lilac gown floating behind her. Heads turned to watch her progress between the tables, with more than one comment passed discreetly from behind a gloved hand.

Madeline appeared not to notice and took her seat with her usual cheerful grin. "I'm so sorry, Cecily. Someone stopped by for one of my potions, and I couldn't turn him away."

"Of course not," Cecily agreed. The general consensus in town was that Madeline's potions were largely consumed by the male population of Badgers End in the hopes of increasing their amorous prowess with the ladies.

While Madeline had never denied that she supplied such assistance, she maintained that her potions cured everything from warts to consumption. Cecily was inclined to give her the benefit of the doubt.

"This is nice," Madeline declared, looking around the cozy room with obvious pleasure. "It has been so long since we have enjoyed a visit here."

Cecily followed her friend's gaze along the decorative plates balanced on the picture rail to the huge fireplace in the corner. China jugs and vases crowded the wide mantelpiece, and a large copper coal scuttle sat in front of the brass fender, hiding the dent from all but the most discriminating eye.

As far as Cecily could tell, the tea shop hadn't changed at all since she used to come there as a small child. Even Dolly looked much the same, with her brown eyes full of laughter and her rolls of fat jiggling as she threaded her way through the tables to reach them.

"Well, it's about time you two ladies came to see me," she said, as she brandished a notebook and pencil. "It is a pleasure to see you again, that it is. What can I get for you this afternoon, Mrs. Sinclair?''

Cecily ordered a pot of tea and sandwiches for two, her stomach growling in anticipation.

''And a tray of cakes?'' Dolly suggested.

Cecily glanced at Madeline, who nodded in resignation. ''Thank you, Dolly, that sounds wonderful. Do you have time to sit down with us for a little while?''

''Tell you what.'' Dolly flipped the notebook shut and slipped it into the wide pocket of her apron. ''As soon as Betsy gets the buns out of the oven, I'll come and have a quick chat with you, all right?''

''We'll look forward to it,'' Cecily assured her.

Dolly started her laborious journey back to the kitchen, and Madeline sighed. ''You know, of course, that all these pastries and cakes are not healthy for your blood.''

Cecily nodded. ''So you've told me. You must admit, Madeline, they do taste awfully good.''

Madeline half closed her beautiful eyes. ''I'll admit it if you tell me why we are really down here.''

''To enjoy a nice pot of tea and crumpets, of course.''

''This has nothing to do with the death of Ivy Glumm, I suppose?''

Cecily made a face at her friend. ''I did think I might ask Dolly about her as long as we are here.''

Madeline shook her head in exasperation, but she smiled anyway. ''I might have known. I will accept any excuse, however, to enjoy an afternoon with you, away from Phoebe's caustic remarks.''

''Phoebe means well, and her bark is worse than her bite, as you well know. Despite her manner, she considers you a good friend.''

''Maybe.'' Madeline leaned forward. ''Now tell me, who do you think murdered poor Ivy Glumm?''

Cecily glanced around to see if anyone was listening, but all the ladies seemed engrossed in their own conversations. ''I have no idea, as yet,'' she said, keeping her voice low, "but it is my considered opinion that the magician knows more than he is saying."

"Why would Denmarric want to kill his assistant?" Madeline murmured.

While Cecily was still trying to decide whether or not to confide in her friend, Madeline's expression changed. "Ivy was having a baby," she whispered.

Half unnerved by Madeline's uncanny power and half relieved that the decision had been taken out of her hands, Cecily nodded.

Madeline tutted. "Poor child."

Cecily gazed thoughtfully at the other woman. Although she had long ago accepted Madeline's ability to perceive beyond the realm of mere mortals, she had never asked her friend to use her powers in order to help in her investigations.

Cecily had a very real fear of dabbling in things she didn't understand, especially those of the occult nature. Having been thoroughly perplexed by this matter of Ivy Glumm, however, she couldn't help wondering if Madeline could shed some light on the subject.

Deciding to take the safest course, she asked casually, "What do you think might have happened?"

"I think that Denmarric might have been dabbling into things that are best left alone. He might have trespassed onto forbidden territory. The spirits get very angry when their domain is invaded. I believe it's possible that Ivy Glumm paid a heavy price for his mistake."

In spite of the warm room, Cecily felt chilled by her words. She might have expected Madeline to answer in that vein, and her practical mind told her that there was a much more logical answer to the puzzle. Yet Madeline's words struck an uneasy chord, and Cecily was vastly relieved when the tea tray arrived and she could concentrate on something a great deal more pleasant.

CHAPTER

❀ 9 ❀

Gertie couldn't wait to get afternoon tea over with in the dining room. It was her evening off, and she planned to spend it in her room, answering the latest letter from Ross while the babies slept at her side.

After stacking the dirty dishes perilously high on the huge tea tray, she carried it from the dining room, intent on getting back to the kitchen as quickly as possible so that Doris could start the washing up.

She'd gone only a few steps down the hallway when she heard Ethel coughing. It wasn't like an ordinary cough. This one seemed to rattle Ethel's teeth as she leaned against the wall, tears streaming down her red face while she struggled desperately to breathe.

"Bloody hell, Ethel, you sound bleeding awful." Gertie rushed forward, heedless of the cups tottering on their precarious perch of stacked saucers.

Ethel's chest heaved as she fought for breath. She held

a handkerchief in one hand, and Gertie's stomach churned when she saw the specks of blood on it.

" 'Ere, Ethel," she whispered, "you'd better get down to the flipping doctor's as fast as you can."

Ethel nodded weakly. "I did," she said, her voice hoarse with coughing.

"Did he give you something?"

Again Ethel nodded.

"It ain't doing no blinking good, is it?"

Ethel shook her head and managed a faint smile. "He said as how it might take a while to work."

Gertie looked at her friend, her heart filling with dread. She'd heard about people coughing like that until they couldn't breathe no more. She couldn't bear the thought of something bad happening to Ethel.

"You need something better than what the doctor give you," she said, trying to keep her voice cheerful so that Ethel wouldn't know how worried she was. "I think we should go to see Madeline Pengrath."

Ethel's eyes opened wide. "We have to go up to her house, you mean?"

"Yeah, it's not far. We can bleeding walk it. We'll go this evening. It's my night off."

"We can't go up to Miss Pengrath's house," Ethel said, sounding scared. "She's a witch, and her house is full of them spirits and ghosts. I don't want to end up buried in the woods like poor Ivy Glumm."

Gertie did her best to ignore the cold shiver down her back. "You're not going to bleeding end up like Ivy Glumm, silly. It were the magician what sent her to the flipping woods to be with the spirits. Miss Pengrath ain't going to send you nowhere, is she? She'll just mix up one of her blinking potions for you, that's all."

Ethel looked even more alarmed at this. "What if she turns me into a toad or something?"

Gertie sighed. Ethel could be such a crybaby sometimes. "She'll give you something to make your bloody cough go away, that's all. Her stuff bleeding works, Ethel. Lots of people swear as how she made them better when the flipping doctor couldn't. You'll see.''

"All right," Ethel said reluctantly. "I'll do anything to get rid of this cough. I'm keeping Joe awake at nights with it. Only you've got to promise me—" She broke off as another fit of coughing choked off her breath.

Gertie waited impatiently for the awful spasms to subside. "Promise you what?" she demanded when Ethel could finally speak again.

"Promise me," Ethel whispered hoarsely, "that if she turns me into a lizard, you'll explain to Joe what happened."

In spite of her worry, Gertie grinned. "If she turns you into a bleeding lizard, I'll have her turn Joe into a blinking lizard, too."

Ethel actually smiled at that. "He wouldn't like that much, would he?" She pushed herself away from the wall, tucked the blood-stained handkerchief into the pocket of her apron, and took off down the hall.

Gertie followed her, praying hard that Miss Pengrath would be able to help her friend. If something bad happened to Ethel, she'd never bleeding get over it. Ethel was her best friend, and there'd never be another one like her. Ethel had to get better again. She just flipping had to.

"Well, now," Dolly said as she hauled a spare chair out from under an adjacent table and set it next to Cecily, "I can spare just a minute or two, that's all. Always busy, I am. Never have a moment to breathe."

"It must be so difficult to find people to help you," Cecily said, offering Dolly a leftover egg and cress sandwich. "I know how hard it is to find staff for the hotel. As it is, I'm thinking of sending Baxter all the way to London to hire a gardener."

"Oh, I know how it is, don't I?" Dolly took the sandwich and stuffed the whole thing into her mouth. She appeared to swallow the entire sandwich before adding, "If it wasn't for Betsy, I would have to cut down the number of tables in here. All our youngsters are going up to London to work. More money, they say. A better life."

"I can't argue with that, I'm afraid." Cecily picked up her cup and saucer. "They don't seem to mind the noise and the smoke."

"The worst of it is the fog," Madeline put in. "Or smog, as they are calling it now. Sometimes it is so thick one has to crawl along the pavement to find the way. People can get lost for hours in it. It really can be quite frightening—like being in the middle of the ocean not knowing in which direction lies the shore."

Dolly shook her head. "Terrible, that's what I say. Still, people have to have their coal fires to keep warm, don't they? Else they'd freeze to death."

"Well, this problem of finding staff is becoming quite desperate," Cecily said, steering the conversation back to where she wanted it. "I imagine you missed Ivy Glumm a great deal after she left."

"Oo, didn't I half?" Dolly's double chins wobbled as she nodded. "Terrible what happened to her, wasn't it? Though nobody seems to know what did happen really." She leaned forward and dropped her voice to a loud whisper. "It's not my place to say, of course, but I reckon that George Dalrymple had something to do with it."

Cecily exchanged a quick glance with Madeline. "I don't think I know him," she said, puckering her forehead. "Does he live in Badgers End?"

"Wellercombe. He works delivery for Barrow's Bakery where I get me flour and baking supplies. That's how Ivy met him." Dolly closed one eye in a conspiratorial wink. "Ivy's boyfriend, he was. Mad as a hornet in a jar of treacle when he found out Ivy was leaving. Came in here waving his arms about and yelling at the top of his voice. Upset all me customers, he did. Some of them walked out without even finishing their tea."

"Oh, dear," Cecily murmured. "How unpleasant."

"You're telling me. He went on and on about how the magician was stealing Ivy away from him, after all the money George had spent on her and everything. Ivy told him that Denmarric was married, and she was only interested in the job because it was glamorous and exciting, but George wouldn't listen."

"Did he threaten her?" Cecily asked, her tea growing cold as she listened to Dolly's story.

Dolly shrugged. "Sort of, I suppose. He said if he couldn't have her, no one else would. Ivy kept saying as how she didn't want the magician, but George stomped out of here, and I haven't talked to him about it since."

"What did Ivy say about all this, after George left, I mean?"

"Nothing much. She was upset, of course. Said as how George had got it all wrong and that she wasn't interested in the magician personal, like, nor him in her. Though I has me doubts about that."

Cecily's interest quickened. "Why do you say that?"

"Oh, I don't know. It's just that the magician already had an assistant when he asked Ivy to work for him. I couldn't think why he would want to change, unless his intentions weren't strictly honorable, so to speak."

"I see," Cecily said, her mind busily absorbing this latest information.

"Anyhow, I'd best be off, or Betsy will be tearing her hair out." Dolly grunted as she heaved her enormous body to her feet. "Don't leave it so long before you come back again, Mrs. Sinclair. You neither, Miss Pengrath. We miss your smiling faces around here, that we do."

Cecily waited until she was out of earshot before commenting, "Well, that was interesting."

Madeline uttered her silvery laugh. "Hot on the trail, as always, Cecily. Poor Inspector Cranshaw doesn't stand a chance, does he?"

"Inspector Cranshaw might stand a better chance, as you

put it, if he pursued the situation, instead of wasting time chasing after other inconsequential matters.'' Cecily reached for the bill, which Dolly had placed surreptitiously on the table, and rose to her feet.

''All I can say to that, dear Cecily,'' Madeline murmured as she, too, rose, ''is to please be cautious. When one is dealing with the supernatural, there can be all kinds of unpleasant consequences.''

In spite of her convictions to the contrary, Cecily couldn't dismiss the thought that if there had been some kind of unearthly intervention in Ivy's demise, it would be terribly hard to prove.

''Are you bleeding coming or not?'' Gertie demanded as she waited on the path to the Downs for Ethel to catch up with her. ''It'll be bloody dark before we get there at this rate.''

''I''m hurrying as fast as I can,'' Ethel said, panting for breath. ''My legs don't work as fast as yours.''

''They bleeding should, seeing as how they haven't got much to carry.'' She hadn't noticed until that moment just how much weight Ethel had lost. She felt a rush of impatience, anxious now to get Ethel into Madeline Pengrath's hands as fast as possible. ''Come *on,* Ethel.''

''I'm coming.'' Ethel reached her and came to a halt, holding her side and puffing like a pair of bellows. ''You know I never could walk as fast as you.''

''Well, it's not much further now.'' Gertie took off again, her long black skirt flapping around her ankles in the brisk wind from the sea.

The sun was going down behind the hills, throwing long shadows across the sands. Gertie felt a stab of nostalgia, remembering how she and Ethel used to chase the seagulls and build sandcastles and laugh themselves silly watching the Punch and Judy shows.

That was before they'd both got married. Those were good days, Gertie thought wistfully. Not that they weren't good now, but things had changed a lot since she was fourteen and had no bleeding worries.

"Wait for me," Ethel said hoarsely. "I've got to catch my breath."

Gertie winced and came to a halt as Ethel started coughing again. The bout seemed to last longer than ever, and Ethel could hardly stand by the time it was over.

"Come on," Gertie said gruffly when Ethel said she was all right again. "Let's go and talk to Miss Pengrath."

Gertie had never been to Madeline Pengrath's house. She'd seen it plenty of times, with its thatched roof and garden thick with strange flowers and bushes.

Standing at the door now, her hand poised to knock, she wondered for a fleeting moment if she was doing the right thing in seeking help from a witch.

But the doctor hadn't done any good, and anyone with half an eye could see Ethel wasn't getting any better. Reassured, Gertie raised her hand and lifted the heavy door knocker.

She had barely let it fall before the door opened, and Miss Pengrath stood there, dressed all in white and looking surprised to see the two housemaids standing on her doorstep.

"Come in," she said when Gertie nervously explained why they were there.

Stepping down into the small, cluttered room, Gertie stared in amazement at the assortment of colorful fabrics, silk flowers, ribbons, laces, and embroidered cushions scattered about the furniture as well as the floor. There didn't seem to be a spot anywhere where she could step without treading on something or other.

She knew that Miss Pengrath sewed articles to sell in the souvenir shops and at fetes, but she never knew she made so much mess doing it. Mrs. Chubb liked to knit, but she always tucked her work in a knitting bag. This place looked like the wind had gone through it and tossed everything in the air. Or maybe it were ghosts, like Ethel said.

She felt Ethel bump into her and realized her friend was shivering violently. Self-consciously, Gertie reached for Ethel's hand and gave it a firm squeeze. "It's all right," she whispered. "You'll be all right."

"Sit down," Miss Pengrath said, waving a hand at some large cushions on the floor. "I only have one chair, so you will have to fight for it."

"Ethel can have the chair," Gertie said, dropping down onto a cushion. "She's the one what's sick."

"So I can see." Miss Pengrath walked up to Ethel and placed her hands on each cheek. "Tell me, my dear, how long have you been like this?"

"I've had this cold for weeks," Ethel said, turning her head as another bout of coughing shook her body.

"She's been to the doctor," Gertie explained, "but his medicine don't seem to do no bleeding good."

"It did go away for a long time," Ethel said quickly, "but it came back again."

"What medicine did the doctor give you?" Miss Pengrath asked.

"I don't know what it's called," Ethel said, turning a dull shade of red. "It's brown cough mixture in a bottle, that's all I know."

"Have you been spitting blood?" Miss Pengrath looked grave when Ethel nodded.

"Just a little, now and then."

"Does your husband know about this?"

Ethel shrugged. "He knows about the cough. It keeps him awake at nights."

"When did you last see the doctor?"

Ethel gave Gertie a guilty look. "Not since I stopped coughing last summer," she muttered.

"You bleeding told me you went back!" Gertie cried, hurt that Ethel hadn't been truthful with her.

Ethel looked at her with frightened eyes. "I was scared to," she whispered. "He told me if the cough came back, I'd have to leave Joe and go away to get better."

Miss Pengrath was silent for so long that Gertie began to get really worried. Then, just when Gertie was about to say something, Miss Pengrath said briskly, "I'll get you something to help with the cough. But you must promise me you will go to see Dr. Prestwick first thing in the morning."

"I'll bleeding make sure that she gets there," Gertie said gruffly.

Miss Pengrath disappeared through a curtain of beads, leaving them clacking together behind her.

Gertie felt terrible when she saw tears in Ethel's eyes.

"I don't want to go away and leave my Joe," she whispered. "What will he do without me?"

"You won't have to go for very long," Gertie said, hoping she was right. "But you have to get bleeding better, Ethel. You won't do your Joe no bloody good if you . . . keep him awake coughing all night."

She couldn't bring herself to voice what was really in her mind. That Ethel might die if she didn't go away. She knew what Ethel had. She didn't need Madeline Pengrath to tell her that Ethel had consumption and that people died from it if they weren't looked after properly.

She was glad now that she'd made Ethel come. She'd make sure she went to the doctor's tomorrow, too. And if Ethel had to go away, well, she'd just have to make sure that she and Joe visited her, that's all.

CHAPTER

✿ 10 ✿

Baxter was not in his office when Cecily went in to see him the next morning, which was something of a relief for her. She had promised him she would not embark on any investigation without advising him of the fact. She knew quite well that if she told him she was going to see George Dalrymple, however, he would insist on accompanying her.

Which was all well and good, but Cecily had the feeling that she would learn more from the young man without Baxter's threatening presence hovering over him. Her manager could be most intimidating at times.

Therefore she felt perfectly justified in leaving a note for Baxter on his desk, informing him of her intended whereabouts. By the time he discovered the note, she would be well on her way to Wellercombe.

Samuel had sent the trap around to the front of the hotel when she stepped out into a gray morning, overcast with dark clouds that promised rain.

She had taken care to wear her serviceable wool coat over her dark blue skirt and white lace-covered blouse. She had fastened a chiffon scarf over her hat and under her chin, a wise precaution, it would seem, in view of the choppy, foam-edged waves rushing to shore ahead of the salty wind.

Cecily accepted the arm of her driver and climbed up into the trap, where she settled herself onto the leather seat with a sigh. It had occurred to her that George Dalrymple, and not the Great Denmarric, could be the father of Ivy's unborn child. It certainly wouldn't be amiss to at least ask him a few questions about Ivy.

After giving her driver the order to drive to Barrow's Bakery, she prepared herself for the long ride. Now that she was on the way, she was beginning to regret not waiting for Baxter to accompany her. She rather missed having him by her side, which surprised her.

She had been alone for so long that her solitude had become customary to her, and sometimes preferable. But now she was beginning to depend on Baxter's presence to fulfill her days, and she wasn't at all sure that was entirely a good thing.

She dismissed her uneasiness and contented herself with watching the world pass until the town of Wellercombe came into view.

The rain pelted down as the trap slowly rolled along the High Street, hemmed in by carriages and the occasional motorcar. Cecily saw the noisy vehicles spray mud over the legs of the passing horses as well as an unsuspecting pedestrian now and again.

Making a mental note to keep away from the curb, she peered through the driving rain at the store windows as they passed by. A display of wedding gowns caught her attention, and her heart skipped a beat.

It would not be suitable for her to wear such a gown, of course, should she ever marry again. Nor was she sure she would want to, even if it were possible. It was the mere thought of being Baxter's wife that had her heart racing and her throat constricted.

The sudden jolt of the trap banished such disturbing thoughts from her mind. Peering up at the sign swaying in the wind, she realized that she had arrived at Barrow's Bakery.

Instructing her driver to wait for her, she entered the large brick building and was greeted by the enticing aroma of freshly baked bread. Crammed into the glass containers all around her were fat loaves of bread, their crusts browned to perfection, as well as round Bath buns, iced Chelsea buns, and enormous Eccles cakes simply bursting with currants and raisins beneath their glittering sugar crust.

Ignoring her pangs of hunger, Cecily asked for George Dalrymple and was politely directed to the rear of the shop, where the smell of baking was positively overpowering.

George Dalrymple was a tall, slender young man with a thick ginger mustache and reddish hair parted neatly in the middle. The white coat he wore reached only to his knees and barely covered his wrists. He seemed surprised but relatively undisturbed when Cecily told him the reason for her visit.

He ushered her into a small sitting room, away from the clatter and whirl of the bakery, although the heavenly fragrance still permeated the air.

In the corner of the room, a dog lay in a frayed basket, its chin on its paws, its dark brown eyes gazing intently at the newcomer. The dog's coat was thick and entirely black, except for a small, uneven cross on its forehead.

The hem of Cecily's skirt whisked past its nose as she passed by its basket, and the dog lifted its head, affronted by the disturbance.

"Lie down, Duke," George said, leaning down to pat the dog's head.

"Is he yours?" Cecily bent down and offered the back of her gloved hand. The dog sniffed it, then gave it a lick.

"Yeah. The owners let me keep him in here while I'm

working. Tears up the place if I leave him at home, and if I leave him outside, he goes off for hours.''

Cecily fondled the dog's ears. ''He seems to like people.''

''He likes the ladies.'' George grinned. ''Follows them around everywhere, he does. Gets to be a nuisance at times.''

''I can imagine.''

''I just saw Ivy the other night,'' George said as Cecily seated herself on a straight-backed chair. ''Did she send you? Is something wrong?''

Wondering if his questions were as innocent as they seemed, Cecily watched his face carefully as she told him how Ivy's body had been discovered.

His shock seemed genuine enough but was quickly replaced by belligerence. '' 'Ere,'' he said, his face reddening, ''I hope you don't think I had anything to do with that. 'Cos you're bloody mistaken if you do.''

''I understand you had a serious argument with Ivy when she told you she was going to work for the Great Denmarric,'' Cecily said, keeping her voice low and calm.

''So what if I did? Besides, that happened bloody months ago. I never set eyes on her again until I saw her at the show the other night. I'll swear to that on the Bible.''

Cecily nodded. ''You saw Ivy get into the box and not come out of it, then.''

''Yeah, we all did, didn't we? I thought at first it were a trick what had gone wrong, but then everyone was saying afterward as how Denmarric had done it on purpose, so's we'd all wonder what happened to her. After all, it were clever, the way he made her disappear.''

He shook his head, muttering almost to himself, '' 'Course, we didn't know she was a stiff'un then.''

''You accused Ivy of having a personal interest in the magician,'' Cecily said. ''In fact, I believe your actual words were that if you couldn't have her, then no one else would either.''

George shrugged. "I lost me temper, that's all. People say all sorts of daft things when they're angry."

"What made you think that Ivy was personally involved with the magician?"

"I dunno, do I? It was just something I said, that's all. I was riled because of all the money I'd spent on her, and she was chucking me because of her new fancy job. Said it wouldn't look right having a delivery boy for a boyfriend, now that she was on the stage."

"She didn't say anything about her feelings toward Denmarric?"

"Nah . . . after I calmed down I reckoned as how she didn't really feel anything about him. She was all excited about being on the stage, that's all." He held out his hands in a gesture of appeal. "Look, Mrs. Sinclair, I was at the show the other night because someone gave me his ticket. I knew as how Ivy was going to be in it, and I was curious. I mean, if I was that angry with her, why would I wait until now to kill her?"

"It could be," Cecily said softly, "that you had just discovered that she was carrying your baby."

George's eyes opened wide as he gave a visible start. "Strewth," he muttered. "It weren't mine, I can swear to that on the Bible, too."

Cecily reached for her umbrella and rose to her feet. "Well, thank you for your time, Mr. Dalrymple. I'm sorry to have been the bearer of such tragic news."

George rushed to open the door for her. "I'd like to know what did happen to her . . . if you find out, I mean . . . you know, who did it, and all."

"I'll see that you're informed." She crossed the floor of the shop, resisting the temptation to buy a bag of buns to eat on the way home. Instead, she concentrated on George's comments, trying to decide if the young man was genuinely upset at the news or just very adept at hiding his guilt.

• • •

Cecily arrived back at the hotel an hour or so later to find Phoebe waiting for her in the library, apparently in a great state of agitation, according to Ned. Baxter had also left a message that he wanted to see her in his office on her immediate return.

Deciding that she would be better able to deal with Baxter if she wasn't worrying about Phoebe waiting for her, Cecily proceeded down the hallway to the library.

Phoebe sat warming her hands by the fire, her face hidden by the sweeping purple plumes of her hat. She tilted her face up as Cecily entered, exclaiming, "Oh, there you are! I've been waiting absolute hours for you."

"I'm sorry, Phoebe. Had I known—"

Phoebe interrupted her with a wave of her pink-gloved hand. "Oh, I know, I should have left my card yesterday when I missed you, but that fool Colonel Fortescue completely took my attention away."

Cecily seated herself on the opposite side of the fireplace and gazed at her friend in concern. "Ned tells me you are extremely put out about something. I sincerely hope the colonel isn't the cause of your distress?"

Phoebe gave an emphatic shake of her head, causing the ostrich feathers on her hat to sweep majestically from side to side. "Not at all. The colonel may be . . . difficult at times, but I really believe the poor man is lonely and desperate for company. What he really needs is a good woman who can take care of him. Heaven knows he can well afford one."

Cecily was taken aback, not so much by Phoebe's unprecedented sympathy for the befuddled gentleman as much as her friend's apparent knowledge of the colonel's financial situation. She hadn't realized that Phoebe had that much interest in the colonel's affairs.

"No," Phoebe continued, "the colonel is not the cause of my concern. My dear Cecily, much as I admire your constraint in this matter, you simply must do something about this dreadful situation in the ballroom. I went down there yesterday to ask the constable on guard how much longer he expected to be there. He was quite rude.''

''I'm sorry, Phoebe. I'll have a word with the inspector when I see him. We can't have his constables being rude to my guests.''

''Dreadful man. His sarcasm was totally uncalled for. All I said was that his presence was interfering with my plans for the tea dance. I told him that I wanted him out of there by the weekend, that our ladies of breeding would be horrified at the thought of entertaining a member of the working class at such a prominent social affair.''

''Oh, dear,'' Cecily murmured, beginning to sympathize with the constable.

''Such a disgusting man.'' Phoebe wrinkled her nose. ''He said it was very inconsiderate of Ivy Glumm to get herself killed on the week of the tea dance. He also said that all I had to do was confess to her murder, and he'd be out of there 'like a . . .' '' she shuddered, then leaned forward and whispered, '' ' . . . like a dog after a bitch in heat.' ''

''Oh, dear,'' Cecily said again.

Phoebe sat back and fanned her face with her handkerchief. ''Can you imagine? Speaking to me in that disgusting manner? The nerve of the man. Why, I shall have a word with the inspector myself and demand that the constable be transferred to the London docks. He wouldn't be quite so brazen when facing some of those louts, you can be sure of that.''

Aware that Phoebe was working herself up into one of her turns, Cecily hastened to smooth her ruffled feathers. ''I'm quite sure the man wasn't aware to whom he was speaking. I'll make certain that it doesn't happen again, Phoebe, I assure you.''

Looking only slightly appeased, Phoebe tucked her handkerchief into her sleeve. ''That's all very well, Cecily, but unless the man is removed, along with all that dreadful clutter littering the stage, we shall have no other recourse but to postpone the tea dance until further notice.''

Cecily wisely refrained from reminding Phoebe that she was largely responsible for ''that dreadful clutter'' in the first place. To be fair, Phoebe was not to blame for what happened to Ivy . . . whatever it was that had happened.

''Cecily, you must solve this dreadful murder yourself if we are to hold the tea dance and fashion presentation as planned. You are so clever at this sort of thing. Not like that fool inspector and that incredibly obtuse constable, Northcott.''

Frustrated by her inability to make any headway in that particular direction, Cecily answered a trifle sharply. ''Phoebe, I would dearly love to solve this puzzle. But I'm afraid that in order to discover who it was murdered Ivy Glumm, I will have to find out exactly how she disappeared in the first place.''

Phoebe tutted. ''Can't you ask Mr. Denmarric? I'm quite sure he would tell you if you explained the emergency of the matter.''

Cecily shook her head. ''I asked him. He refuses to divulge the secret.''

''Well, what about that dreadful woman, Charlotte Watkins? She's Mr. Denmarric's wife—surely she should know how the trick was done.''

''Possibly.'' Cecily glanced up at the clock. ''As a matter of fact, the same thought had occurred to me. While I was in Wellercombe this morning, I stopped by to see Charlotte. I invited her to join me for afternoon tea here at the hotel. I thought she would have less chance to end the conversation prematurely if I was entertaining her in my suite instead of attempting to question her in her own home.''

Phoebe looked horrified. ''You invited her here for tea? Whatever are you thinking of, Cecily? Do you have any idea how demeaning it would be if anyone saw you entertaining such a lowly creature?''

''No more demeaning than having to explain why we

had to cancel the tea dance,'' Cecily said dryly.

Phoebe coughed politely behind her hand. ''Well, we . . . er . . . wouldn't have to say exactly why, would we?''

Cecily raised her eyebrows in mock surprise. ''You would have me lie to our guests?''

''Well, not lie, exactly . . .'' Phoebe waved her hand in the air. ''More a matter of avoiding a full explanation, I suppose.''

Cecily shook her head. ''I was rather hoping it wouldn't come to that. Nevertheless, unless I can discover how Denmarric caused Ivy to disappear, I'm afraid you are right, Phoebe. We shall have to postpone the tea dance. Time is running out on us. In fact, if I am no closer to solving this puzzle by tomorrow, I shall have to send out the announcements.''

''Well, now that you have a telephone, that task should be easier.'' Phoebe rose, smoothing her fingers up her elbow-length gloves before reaching for her umbrella. ''I just pray that you are successful in learning something from that awful woman. Although in my opinion it is a miracle she had enough intelligence to understand how any of her husband's feats were performed.''

Cecily rose, too, aware that she had only a few minutes to spend with Baxter before Charlotte was due to arrive. ''I'll be sure to inform you of any further developments and if we are forced to cancel our plans.''

''Oh, I do hope not. I shall have to reschedule the pianist, as well as the entire fashion presentation. It was quite difficult to organize it all, and soon the season will be on us, and the fashions will be passé. You know how quickly they change.''

''I don't think this season's summer gowns will have gone out of fashion in a month or two,'' Cecily said soothingly.

''One never knows nowadays. The French are constantly surprising us lately, and I'm very much afraid that much of England will eventually adopt their dreadful mode of dress. Have you seen their latest gowns? Flat bodices and no waist . . . not to mention the scandalous length of the skirt . . . quite disgraceful, I call it.''

''I'm sure it will be some time before the English are quite as daring,'' Cecily assured her as she opened the door for her friend.

''I hope you are right, Cecily.'' Phoebe paused in the doorway. ''By the way, you never did tell me how Ivy died. Not that I want all the gory details, of course, but I did wonder how she was killed.''

''No one seems to know. Her heart simply stopped beating.''

''Oh, my! You don't suppose she died of fright, do you? I've heard that's quite possible, you know.''

Cecily raised her eyebrows. ''That hadn't occurred to me, actually, but it's certainly something to consider.''

''Well, I do hope that awful woman tells you what you want to know. I, for one, would dearly love to know how the illusion was performed. I can't imagine how Ivy got out of that box without me seeing her. I was standing right in front of the stage, for heaven's sake.''

''Perhaps we'll both have our curiosity satisfied soon.''

''Perhaps, though there are so many odd things to be explained. All this talk of evil spirits and no one knowing how the poor girl died. Something inhuman about it, if you ask me.''

Cecily watched her leave, Phoebe's last words unsettling her more than she cared to admit. Much as she respected Madeline and her mysterious powers, she couldn't bring herself to believe that some ghostly phantom had spirited Ivy Glumm away and neatly buried her in the woods on Putney Downs.

She was quite certain that whoever had buried Ivy had also killed her. But who? And how? All she really had to go on was speculation and suspicions.

Phoebe was right. There were so many questions left unanswered, with little means of finding the answers unless

Charlotte Watkins was willing to share her husband's secrets.

Walking down to Baxter's office, Cecily debated in her mind the best way to bring up the subject. She was still pondering the question when a voice said wryly, "I assume that George Dalrymple did not confess to the murder?"

She looked up to see Baxter waiting for her in the doorway, wearing a formidable frown. Her stab of guilt inexplicably annoyed her. "You assume correctly. I did leave you a note as to my whereabouts, as I promised."

He waited until she was inside his office before saying somewhat sternly, "A note would hardly have been much help had you met with antagonism while questioning a suspected murderer."

Cecily sank onto a chair, aware that her irritation stemmed more from her frustrated efforts than anything he might have said. She made an effort to curb her resentment. "I'm sorry, Baxter. But you weren't here when I came in this morning, and I was anxious to talk to George Dalrymple before he left the bakery. I felt it would be safer there than at his home."

Baxter sat down at his desk, his expression softening just a little. "I was worried about you, Cecily. I have no wish to dictate your actions to you or control your life. I merely want to be allowed to offer my protection should the need arise. I thought that was understood between us."

Her resentment melted away at once. "Of course it is understood, Bax. If I'd had the slightest doubt about my safety, I would certainly have tracked you down and asked you to accompany me." She gave him a tentative smile. "I did rather miss you, actually."

"Is that supposed to compensate for my deep concern about your safety?"

"I suppose not." She sighed. "It won't happen again, Bax. I promise. In fact, I might as well tell you now that I am entertaining Denmarric's wife for afternoon tea in my suite this afternoon for the sole purpose of questioning her about her husband's illusions. You are quite welcome to join us, should you so desire.''

He shook his head. ''Thank you, but I'll gracefully decline. I find it difficult to believe that Mrs. Watkins could have killed Ivy Glumm, since she was never out of sight of the audience.''

''Neither was Denmarric,'' Cecily reminded him, ''and yet he remains one of my firm suspects.''

''This is causing you a great deal of exasperation, I can tell,'' Baxter said, sounding more sympathetic.

''I can honestly say that this is the most puzzling situation I have ever encountered,'' Cecily admitted.

''Well, perhaps Mrs. Watkins can shed some light on the mystery.''

''I certainly hope so, Baxter.'' Cecily wearily rose to her feet. ''If not, the Pennyfoot will face a substantial loss in revenue. Not only that, our reputation will suffer, and that is something we can ill afford.'' She looked at him, feeling utterly helpless for once. That worried her most of all.

CHAPTER

❧ 11 ❧

Charlotte Watkins arrived promptly at three, looking unusually demure in a natural linen two-piece suit, the jacket
of which, Cecily was intrigued to notice, was semifitted. It
would seem as if Phoebe's concerns about the French fashions could be well founded.

Actually, Cecily thought as she ushered the other woman
toward her velvet winged armchair, she personally would
welcome the looser fitting clothes. She had long ago fallen
into the habit of abandoning her corset whenever she was
alone in her suite.

She wondered what Baxter would say to that if he knew
and felt her cheeks growing warm at the provocative
thought.

"It's so-o-o nice of you to invite me, Mrs. Sinclair,"
Charlotte gushed in a high-pitched affected tone that had
obviously been diligently practiced.

"My pleasure, Mrs. Watkins." Cecily reached for the bell pull and gave it a sharp tug.

"Oh, please, address me as Charlotte. Mrs. Watkins makes me feel so ancient."

"Charlotte, then. The tea should arrive in a minute or two. I trust your journey from Wellercombe was pleasant?"

"Quite pleasant, thank you." Charlotte gazed around the room, her face avid with curiosity. "What's that thing over there?" she asked, pointing a finger at the fireplace.

"It's an elephant tusk. A gift to my husband from an African chief."

"Oo, my," Charlotte muttered, abandoning her feigned accent. "Big bugger, weren't it?"

"It was, indeed," Cecily agreed.

A light tap on the door announced the arrival of the tea. Doris entered the room bearing a large silver tray loaded down with a silver tea service, a three-tiered plate of small triangular sandwiches with their crusts neatly removed, and an enticing assortment of cakes and pastries that widened Charlotte's eyes.

"Will that be all, mum?" Doris asked after unloading the heavy tray.

"Thank you, Doris. That will be all for now."

"Yes, mum." Doris dropped a curtsey, then backed out of the door.

Cecily waited until Charlotte had apparently had her fill of the food before attempting to bring the conversation around to Denmarric. It was Charlotte herself who gave Cecily the opening she needed.

"Never could eat this stuff when I was on stage with me husband," she explained as she reached for yet another Swiss tart. "I had to stay thin to get into them costumes. I don't have to worry so much now that I'm only helping out with the props, like."

"That must have been exciting for you, working on the stage with your husband," Cecily said, offering her the cake plate again.

Charlotte looked longingly at the two cakes left on the plate, then reluctantly shook her head. "I've ate too much already," she said, rubbing a hand over her stomach. "I'll bloomin' pop if I eat any more."

Cecily replaced the plate on the table. "How did you meet your husband, then?"

Charlotte covered her mouth with her hand to smother a soft belch. "Oo, pardon me, I'm sure," she murmured. "Actually, I met Dennis on the stage. I mean, I wasn't married to him when I first started working for him. That sort of happened a bit later on. He wasn't the Great Denmarric then, neither. He changed his name when he got popular."

Cecily nodded. "He's a very clever magician."

"Yeah, he is that. Mind you, he works hard, and he's really particular about everything on stage. He spends an awful lot of money on his props and costumes. Buys his assistants a new outfit for every performance, he does. Lucky he had a spare costume the other night; else I'd have had to go on in me ballgown."

"Well, I would say that the expense is well spent. Your husband is very successful."

"Yeah, he's good, all right. Too bad he ain't as good at being a husband. I have to keep me eye on him, like, if you know what I mean. 'Course, it's hard on him, having all those ladies in the audience falling over him. Mind you, not much gets past me. I don't allow no hanky-panky. Specially with those assistants of his. They're always getting the wrong ideas, they are. Stupid little buggers."

Cecily wondered if perhaps Charlotte had known about Ivy's condition. If so, it might have given her good reason to get rid of the assistant. Then again, Charlotte was also highly visible that night.

"It must be quite difficult to find a good assistant," she said, reaching for the teapot. "Another cup of tea?"

"No, thank you. Actually, I'd say it was near impossible to find a good one. Look at this last one, Ivy Glumm. Flipping useless, she was. Not that I want to talk ill of the dead, mind you. But I might have known she'd go and get herself in trouble one day.''

"Oh?" Cecily murmured casually. "What was it that made you think so?"

Charlotte licked her fingers, then wiped them on her serviette. "Well, she was stupid for one thing. Made lots of mistakes. Same as the one he had before, Jasmine Hicks. She weren't no better. Dennis dropped her before the Christmas season because she weren't no good. Then he gets lumbered with Ivy Glumm.''

"Has your husband found a replacement for Ivy yet?"

"No, nor is he likely to. I'll probably have to be his assistant again, at least until he finds someone else. If he ever does."

"What about this Jasmine Hicks? Would she work with him again?"

Charlotte shook her head. "Nah, she's out of the business, ain't she? Works for Dr. Rodgers, the dentist in Wellercombe now. No, I think Dennis will just have to put up with me again. Who knows, he might even decide there ain't no one better than his wife up there with him?"

"It would certainly solve some problems," Cecily said thoughtfully.

"None of them ever come up to me, anyhow," Charlotte said, crushing her serviette into a ball. "When I was up there with Dennis, we had the whole place enthralled, we did. Dennis always said as how I was his right hand, and he couldn't do the act without me."

She sighed, dropping the crumpled linen onto her plate. "Then we got married, didn't we? Things just weren't the same on stage for us after that, and in the end Dennis said as how it didn't look right to have his wife up there with him. So he has me help him with the props now."

She looked up at Cecily, a fierce scowl on her face. "I can still do better than any of them up there. Even after all this time, I haven't forgotten nothing. I proved that the other night, didn't I?''

''You certainly did,'' Cecily assured her. ''In fact, I'm quite sure had it been you inside that box instead of Ivy when she disappeared, your husband would have succeeded in completing the illusion.''

Charlotte looked wary. ''I don't know about that. Something strange happened there, didn't it? I don't know what happened. I do know one thing, though. It weren't my Dennis's fault, that it weren't. It ain't right that the bobbies are holding all his stuff here. He ain't done nothing wrong. I was there the whole time, and he didn't lay a finger on Ivy Glumm. I can swear to that.''

''Nevertheless, someone did,'' Cecily said quietly. ''And until the police find out exactly what happened to her, naturally they don't want anything moved.''

''Well, I wish they'd flipping hurry up, that's all I can say. Dennis has another week's engagement in Wellercombe next week, and if he don't get his stuff back soon, he'll have to cancel the performances. That won't look good on his record, now will it?''

''I can assure you, Charlotte, I am just as anxious to have this matter cleared up.'' Cecily paused, then added casually, ''Perhaps if you could tell me how Ivy left the box without anyone seeing her, we could piece something together that might help us find out who killed her.''

Charlotte brushed some errant crumbs off her lap. ''I'm sorry, Mrs. Sinclair, but I'm sworn to secrecy. It's more than my life's worth to tell you how Dennis does his tricks. If you want to know how he made Ivy Glumm vanish, you'll have to ask him yourself. He's the only one what could tell you. And I wouldn't hold out too much hope of that happening. There ain't nothing in this world more closely guarded than the secrets of a magician's illusions.''

''Not even if it meant risking a week's engagement at the Hippodrome?''

Charlotte shook her head. ''Not even for that. All I can

say is that some things aren't what they seem. What you see isn't always what really happens. Like they say, not every rose smells as sweet as it looks.''

Realizing that it was useless to pursue the matter, Cecily gracefully brought the visit to an end. She was anxious now to put her new telephone to good use. She needed to make an appointment with a dentist.

Phoebe had not left the hotel after leaving the library. She had fully intended to go home, but halfway across the foyer it occurred to her that since there was only one constable on guard in the ballroom, sooner or later he would have to excuse himself in order to take care of . . . certain personal matters.

In which case, Phoebe assured herself, she would have plenty of time to examine the box from which Ivy disappeared.

She was surprised that Cecily hadn't thought of that. In fact, she turned herself around with the idea of returning to the library to ask Cecily to accompany her.

But then she remembered that Cecily had an engagement with that dreadful woman, Charlotte Watkins, and most likely would not be free for an hour or more. By then, the opportunity could well be lost.

Phoebe wasn't quite sure when the constable would be relieved by his replacement, but she imagined it would be after the late supper.

Glancing at the grandfather clock, she estimated that afternoon tea would be over by now, and the ballroom would be empty until the maids prepared the tables for the evening meal. This was probably the only opportunity she would have to slip unnoticed onto the stage and look inside the box.

She had no idea what she expected to find. She did know that any delay in discovering who had killed that poor child would effectively destroy her arrangements for the tea dance and fashion presentation. Phoebe did not like to be thwarted in her carefully laid plans.

If there was anything at all in that box to indicate who might have done this dastardly deed, then Phoebe would ferret it out. Cecily had seemed quite certain that once she knew how the illusion was done, she would be able to ascertain who had murdered Ivy Glumm. Phoebe intended to uncover that vital piece of information, and as soon as possible.

On the landing above her head, Colonel Fortescue watched the petite woman dither back and forth in front of the grandfather clock. He was absolutely fascinated with her graceful movements, reminded of a figurine in a musical box he'd seen once while in India.

Mrs. Carter-Holmes was a delicate woman, with eggshell skin and a nipped-in waist that he would dearly love to cradle in his hands. She was always so immaculately dressed, with her graceful skirts, high buttoned shoes, long kid gloves, and those magnificent hats of hers.

By Jove, she was a fine figure of a woman, no doubt about that. A man would be damn proud to have her by his side. In fact, the colonel was beginning to think quite seriously about that possibility.

He would have to plan a course of action, naturally. After all, one didn't just go barging up to a woman and announce that one's intentions were serious. And it wasn't as if Mrs. Carter-Holmes had a father to whom he could present his objective.

Fortescue twirled the end of his mustache with fingers that had begun to tremble with excitement. He could, of course, approach her son on the matter. A second later he dismissed the idea. Rotten thinking, that. The blighter was a vicar. And a little bit odd, at that.

Fortescue just couldn't see himself explaining to the Reverend Algernon Carter-Holmes that he was interested in bedding his mother. Even if he did intend to ask for her hand in marriage.

No, the way to corner this little filly was to take it one step at a time. Military tactics, that was it. Plan the strategy, play the game, and all that rot, what?

Fortescue scratched his beard, his gaze still firmly fixed on Phoebe. First things first, he decided. He had to gain her confidence. Charm her, so to speak. Get her so dashed dizzy with delight that she wouldn't know if she was coming or going. Then he'd invite her to dinner.

Yes, that was it! By George, this was going to be jolly good fun, what?

Excitement made him heady for a moment, and he closed his eyes to steady his whirling senses. When he opened his eyes again, Phoebe had vanished.

Determined not to be robbed of his objective, Fortescue charged for the stairs and began lumbering down them at a rather dangerous speed. He curbed the impulse to shout out her name. Something told him she would not appreciate him bellowing after her like some bawdy costermonger.

Halfway down he missed his footing and almost fell headlong down the stairs. Fortunately his flailing arm hit the banister, sending him crashing into the railings. He made a wild grab at the slats and managed to steady himself.

Unnerved by his near miss, he walked carefully down the last few steps to the foyer. Once there, he had to think a moment or two before he remembered what he'd been in such a blasted rush about.

Casting his gaze about the place, he caught a glimpse of blue silk skirt whisking around the far corner of the hallway. Of course, he'd been in hot pursuit of the Carter-Holmes woman.

Putting his head down, he charged along the hallway, his mind vaguely registering that Phoebe was heading toward the ballroom and would have to pass by the bar.

He was faced with a choice, and what a predicament, by Jove. He could abandon the chase and console himself with a gin or two, or he could blast full steam ahead and accomplish his mission. If he could remember what his mission was.

He pulled up short, then snapped his fingers in the air. Of course! Charm the lady, then invite her to dinner. That was it. Perish the thought of gin. The bar would still be there when he returned. Whereas, if he didn't look sharp and get a blasted move on, Phoebe would have disappeared from sight. It could be days before he got such a marvelous opportunity again.

Reaching the closed doors of the ballroom, Fortescue paused to draw a deep breath. Wouldn't do to rush in there panting like a thirsty terrier. Dignity, that's what these woman liked. Calm and dignified, that's what he'd show her.

Giving his mustache a final twirl, he advanced on the door. Slowly he pushed it open and peeked in. The sight of the ribbon barriers gave him a start. He'd forgotten about all that nonsense with the constabulary guard. He couldn't even remember why it was there, except that it had something to do with the magic show he'd watched the other night.

His gaze fell on the constable, snoring on a chair in front of the stage. Fortescue uttered a snort of disgust. These policemen nowadays didn't know the first thing about keeping watch. Jolly good job the blighter wasn't in his regiment during the Boer War. He'd have his blasted head shot off for sleeping on duty.

In fact, Fortescue thought, in growing indignation, he'd a blasted good mind to go in there and give the chap the toe of his boot. Damn disgusting it was, sleeping on watch, indeed.

He was about to do just that when a slight movement caught his eye—a flash of blue silk in the far corner, tucked behind one of the wide stone pillars.

Fortescue blinked and blinked again. His eyesight was a little fuzzy, but he could swear . . . He squinted, bringing the shadows into focus. By Jove, it *was* Phoebe Carter-

Holmes, skulking behind the pillar as if she didn't want to be discovered.

She kept peeking around the white column at the sleeping constable across the room. Fortescue shook his head. What in blazes was she up to? That's what he wanted to know.

He had more or less decided to go in there and ask her when the constable suddenly yawned loudly and stretched his arms over his head.

Fortescue saw Phoebe duck behind the pillar, out of sight. Looking back at the policeman, he realized that the man was heading straight for him—or rather, the doors.

Instinctively the colonel flattened himself against the wall. The constable barged out into the hallway and ran for the bar, without even looking around.

Pleased with his clever strategy, Fortescue opened the door and slipped quietly inside the ballroom. His gaze went immediately to the pillar where Phoebe was hidden. He could see no sign of her from there, and he started forward, intent on getting to her before the constable returned and discovered him lurking around. Could be dashed embarrassing, that.

He'd taken no more than a step or two before a movement in front of the stage attracted his attention. There was the lady of his dreams, stooping to duck under the barriers. Before he could make a sound, she hurried up the front steps to the stage.

Now he knew that something extremely odd was going on. Phoebe Carter-Holmes was an honorable woman. One of the most honorable women that he knew. She would never lower herself to skulk around in such a furtive manner unless she had a desperate goal in mind.

Colonel Fortescue wanted very badly to know what that was. He kept his gaze fixed on Phoebe as she approached one of the boxes that had been left there by the magician. So intent was he on not missing a single movement that he even forgot to blink.

He saw Phoebe toss a glance over her shoulder in his direction. He froze, not wanting to interrupt her quest until he knew what it was. He must have been hidden in the shadows, however, since she didn't appear to see him.

He waited, holding his breath in an agony of suspense in case the constable should return and catch Phoebe in the act. He imagined jumping the man, holding him down until the object of his affection could escape. He could always say that he thought the constable was an intruder.

With his gaze still firmly fastened on Phoebe, Fortescue moved to his right to get a better view. He saw Phoebe open the door of the box and peer inside. For some reason, he began to get an uneasy gnawing feeling under his belt.

He wanted to step forward and call out to her. He didn't know why but he had the odd feeling that she was in some kind of terrible danger.

So strong was his feeling that he actually held up his hand, but just then Phoebe stepped inside the box. The door closed slowly behind her.

Fortescue stood there as the agonizing moments ticked by. He felt dizzy, and little black spots danced before his eyes. He suddenly realized he'd been holding his breath too long and let it out on a rush.

He kept staring at the box, willing Phoebe to come out. What the devil could she be doing in there? It was hardly big enough for her to turn around in, leave alone do anything else.

He waited . . . and waited.

Still she didn't appear. Any second now the constable was going to show up. What was he going to tell him? That Phoebe was stuck inside the box? For surely she must be, or she would certainly have been out again by now.

Suddenly galvanized into action, Fortescue hurried forward to the rescue. He had to get his lady out of there and, with any luck, out of the room before the policeman came back and caught her in the act.

Charging up the steps, he prayed he wouldn't fail in his

mission. This was his very first opportunity to show his fair
lady the stuff he was made of, and by Jove, he wasn't going
to let her down now.

Finally reaching the box, Fortescue drew a shuddering
breath of relief. Any minute now and he'd have her out of
there. Envisioning her grateful cries of joy and admiration,
he smiled as he threw open the door.

His smile froze on his face. The box was quite empty.
Phoebe had apparently vanished into thin air.

CHAPTER

❈ 12 ❈

"Thank you so much for seeing me on such short notice," Cecily said as the slender young lady ushered her into the long, narrow cubicle. "I do hope this isn't too much of an inconvenience."

"Not at all, Mrs. Sinclair. May I have your hat?"

Cecily unpinned her hat, took it off, and handed it to the assistant.

"Now, if you'll just sit in this chair? Dr. Rodgers will be in to see you in just a tick."

"Thank you. Jasmine, isn't it?" Cecily leaned back in the leather chair, closing her eyes briefly as a sharp flash of light reflected off a small, square machine standing on a table nearby. "It's a pretty name. So unusual."

The girl's scrawny face flushed. "Well, it's not really my name. I got called that when I was on the stage. I liked it, though, so I kept it."

"Ah, I thought I'd seen you somewhere before. The Hippodrome, wasn't it?"

Jasmine seemed reluctant to answer. She busied herself tying a bib around Cecily's neck before saying rather sulkily, "That's right. I was once assistant to the Great Denmarric, the magician."

"Oh, really?" Cecily raised her eyebrows in feigned surprise. "Well, fancy that. The magician recently appeared at my hotel, the Pennyfoot in Badgers End."

"Well, I never." Jasmine's voice held a tinge of sarcasm. "He does get around in his tea half hour, doesn't he?"

Cecily smiled. "It sounds as if you don't care for the gentleman."

Jasmine turned her back and began laying out instruments on a white cloth. "I don't like him much," she muttered.

"He seems to be quite a remarkable magician." Eyeing the frail figure of the dental assistant, Cecily wondered if Denmarric had a penchant for skinny women.

"Oh, he's good, all right. Too bloomin' good. He thinks he's God Almighty, he does."

There was no mistaking the bitterness in Jasmine's voice now. Cecily eased herself higher up the chair. "Some of his illusions are quite extraordinary." She hesitated, wondering if Jasmine had heard about Ivy's death. Although Wellercombe was less than twenty miles away from Badgers End, it was a big town, and news did not travel as swiftly among the residents as in the village.

While she was still making up her mind whether or not to mention the murder, Jasmine said stiffly, "Not if you know how they're done. It's like all those tricks, isn't it? Once you know how it's done, it's easy."

"Ah, but that's where the skill of the magician is important, in fostering the illusion so that it appears to be difficult, if not impossible."

"Yeah, well, like I said, I know how it's all done." She

turned back to Cecily, and her face held no expression. "You need to shift down a bit, Mrs. Sinclair, so's Dr. Rodgers can look inside your mouth. Now, which side did you say was hurting?"

"The left side," Cecily said, patting her cheek. "It must have been quite exciting, I imagine, working with a magician on the stage."

Jasmine shrugged. "I s'pose so."

"What made you decide to give it up?"

This time Cecily saw a flash of resentment in Jasmine's dark eyes. "I didn't give it up, did I?" she said, her voice low and intense. "He bleeding sacked me. Said as how I wasn't doing the tricks right. But I knew he only wanted to get rid of me so's *she* could be his assistant."

"She?"

"That Ivy Glumm. Right little tart she was. I could tell she weren't no good, and I told him so. He wouldn't listen to me, though. He fancied her, you see, and that was all he cared about."

Cecily nodded in sympathy. "That must have been very upsetting for you."

"It were, I can tell you. What really upset me was, I couldn't get another job on the stage after that. I used to be a really good acrobat before I met Dennis. I could hold up five people on me shoulders without trembling."

"My," Cecily murmured, impressed in spite of herself. "That must have been quite a feat."

Jasmine shrugged. "I'm stronger than I look. It's all in the training, you see. But then when Dennis sacked me, everyone thought I was a troublemaker. That's why I had to take this job. Mind you, it pays better. That Dennis Watkins is a stingy miser, all right. Wouldn't save his mother's life for a farthing, he wouldn't."

"That surprises me," Cecily said, pretending to look shocked. "He seems such a nice man. And such a brilliant magician. His vanishing lady act, for instance, is breathtaking. I wonder how he does that?"

"Lots of people would like to know that one." Jasmine picked up the water jug. "You'd be surprised how many people have asked me about it."

Cecily turned her head so that she could see the dental assistant's face. "I suppose you have heard that something went wrong the night Denmarric performed the illusion at the Pennyfoot?"

Malicious pleasure shone in Jasmine's face. "Something went wrong? Go on! What happened, then?"

"The magician succeeded in making Ivy Glumm disappear. Unfortunately she failed to return."

This time Jasmine's expression registered shock. "Blimey! What happened to her?"

"Ivy was found the next day. Someone had buried her body in the woods on Putney Downs."

"Gawd!" Jasmine clutched her throat. "Who did it, then?"

"The police are investigating the murder, but so far I haven't heard how successful they have been." Obviously the girl didn't hold with the belief that Ivy had been spirited away by supernatural beings, Cecily noted.

"Strewth! I didn't like the girl, but I wouldn't want to wish that on her," Jasmine muttered, looking shaken.

"I'm sure no one would, except the person who killed her, of course."

"I'm glad I'm not working for him now. That could've been me. Just goes to show, you never really know when you're well off." Jasmine hurried over to the door. "I'll get you some water, Mrs. Sinclair. Dr. Rodgers will be in to see you directly."

"It's a pity you weren't at the performance that night," Cecily said as Jasmine opened the door. "Denmarric had to press his wife into service. Had you been there, you could have taken Ivy's place."

Jasmine looked back at her. "No, thank you, Mrs. Sinclair. I've had it with the stage. It's a hard life. And I wouldn't go near Denmarric the Dreadful again if my life depended on it. I haven't seen him since the day he threw me out, and good riddance to him, that's what I say."

The door closed behind her, leaving Cecily alone. She sat for a long, tedious time waiting for the dentist to attend to her. In fact, she got quite irritated when she heard laughter from the next room. She didn't think it was at all amusing for the dentist to keep her waiting while he had such an entertaining time.

When he finally put in an appearance, Dr. Rodgers apologized profusely for his tardiness, explaining that he'd been dealing with a "difficult" patient.

After examining Cecily's teeth, he informed her she needed some work done on them and suggested she set up another appointment.

Cecily had no intention of traveling all the way back to Wellercombe for such an inconsiderate dentist. The deficient state of her teeth, however, would at least provide her with a legitimate reason for being there, Cecily thought as she left. Perhaps now Baxter wouldn't be quite so put out by the fact that she had once more neglected to inform him of her whereabouts.

"Well, what do you bloody think!" Gertie exclaimed as she rushed into the kitchen. "Now it's Mrs. Carter-Holmes what's gone and disappeared. The bobby's right bleeding upset, I can tell you. Happened right in front of his bloody nose."

Mrs. Chubb looked up from the mound of pastry, her fingers busily digging and folding. "What are you talking about, girl?"

Gertie paused to get her breath back, her hand over her chest. "Mrs. Carter-Holmes. She got inside that flipping magician's box what was standing on the stage, and now she's disappeared."

Mrs. Chubb's fingers stilled as she stared at Gertie. "Who told you that?"

"Doris. She heard the bloody constable yelling at old Fortescue."

Mrs. Chubb shook her head in bewilderment. "What's the colonel got to do with all this?"

"He was the one what found her missing. He told the constable she went in there and didn't come out again."

"That's nonsense and you know it. You know how confused Colonel Fortescue gets and how everyone tries to avoid him. More than likely he saw Mrs. Carter-Holmes near the box, and she slipped out before he could catch up with her. You should know better, Gertie Brown, than to believe anything that poor gentleman says. Now get on with folding those serviettes, or we'll be late getting the tables set up for dinner."

Gertie shrugged. "It's not me what believes the old fool, it's the bleeding constable. Last I heard, he wanted to take the colonel down to the station for questioning."

"Well, I think it's all a great big fuss about nothing," Mrs. Chubb declared, pressing her rolling pin into the mound of pastry on her board. "I can't understand why that constable is being so nasty with Colonel Fortescue. Why, everyone around here knows the old gentleman is harmless."

"He may be bloody harmless to you," Gertie muttered as she picked up another serviette to fold, "but there's more than one housemaid around here who has to watch her bleeding bum when he comes by."

"Watch your tongue, Gertie Brown," Mrs. Chubb snapped, wagging her rolling pin at Gertie. "Colonel Fortescue might act a bit strange at times, but we must remember he is a guest in this hotel and deserves respect."

"Strange?" Gertie uttered a sarcastic laugh. "The poor bugger's bleeding daffy. Everybody knows that."

"That's as may be. But the constable has no reason to treat him so poorly. Just wait until madam gets back and finds out what's been going on. She'll be that upset . . ." Mrs. Chubb clicked her tongue. "Sometimes I wonder how that poor woman puts up with all this trouble.''

"She's a strong woman," Gertie said, slapping another folded serviette onto the growing pile in front of her. "I really admire the way she stands up to everyone like she does. Wish I had her money. I'd give some of them blokes bleeding what for, I would."

Mrs. Chubb lifted her chin and wiped the back of her hand across her perspiring forehead. "What are you talking about, Gertie? What blokes . . . men, I mean?"

Gertie tossed her head. "Them blokes what think it's their blinking duty to order women about and tell them what to bleeding do all the time."

"Like who, in particular?"

"They all do it, don't they? You want to hear some of them flipping toffs leading off at their wives. Flipping heck, you'd think they was little children the way they talk to them sometimes. I wouldn't let no blinking man talk to me like that if I had bleeding money, I'll tell you."

"What does money have to do with it, then?"

Gertie sighed. "If you have money, you don't need no men, now, do you? You can tell 'em all to sod off, can't you?"

Mrs. Chubb frowned. "What's got you all in a dither, then? That Ross McBride giving you trouble, then?"

Gertie could feel her cheeks growing red at the mention of his name. Staring hard at the serviette in her hand, she muttered, "No, he ain't."

"Then who is it put your nose out of joint?"

"No one. I'm just flipping upset about something, that's all," Gertie muttered, wishing she hadn't started this conversation.

"About what?"

"Nothing."

There was a long pause; then Mrs. Chubb laid down her rolling pin. "Gertie Brown, are you going to tell me, or do I have to drag it out of you?"

"I'm not supposed to say anything," Gertie blurted out.

"Ethel made me promise." To her dismay her voice broke, and she thought she was going to cry. She swallowed hard and went back to folding the serviette.

She could tell Mrs. Chubb was staring at her. Then after a minute or two the housekeeper said quietly, "If something has happened to Ethel that I should know about, then it's your duty to tell me, Gertie. It doesn't have to go any further."

Gertie looked up and tried to stop her voice from sounding funny when she said, "All right, then. Ethel's got flipping consumption."

Mrs. Chubb's face grew as white as the flour dusting her apron. "Oh, my," she whispered. "I thought as much. I was going to tell madam about it, but I couldn't bring myself to, knowing what she'd say and all."

Gertie nodded. "I know. Ethel went to see the doctor today. He says as how Ethel has to go to a blinking sanna . . . something."

"Sanitarium," Mrs. Chubb supplied.

"Yes, that's it. Anyway, it's like a hospital where she has to stay to get better. He told her that she could spread her germs around if she stayed here and make us all bleeding sick."

"That she could." Mrs. Chubb's hand strayed to her throat. "Poor little mite. She must be terrified. When does she have to go?"

Gertie could feel a lump coming up in her throat and swallowed it down again. "That's just it. She says she's not going. She won't leave Joe alone. I think she's scared she won't bleeding come back if she leaves."

"Oh, Gertie, she'll die if she doesn't go. She could give it to Joe as well."

Gertie nodded. "I know. I told her. I was there when she told Joe and . . ." She took a deep breath. "He cried. He said he couldn't manage without her. That's why she said she couldn't go."

"Well, we'll just have to talk some sense into her when

she comes in tomorrow," Mrs. Chubb said briskly.

"She ain't coming in tomorrow." To Gertie's embarrassment, she could feel a big fat tear rolling down her cheek. "She says she's not coming back, 'cause she doesn't want to give us all her blinking germs. She didn't want me to tell anyone. She's writing a letter to madam to say she doesn't want to bloody work here no more."

"Oh, my." Mrs. Chubb shook her head. "Well, we have to do something. I'll have a word with madam in the morning. Maybe she can do something with her."

"I bleeding hope so." Gertie gulped. "I know I promised her I wouldn't tell, but I'm so bloody scared she's going to die. If you could have seen the two of them, holding each other and crying . . . it bleeding broke me heart, it did. I don't know what's flipping worse, knowing she's going to die if she stays or knowing how bloody awful it will be for both of them if she goes away."

She was crying in earnest now, the tears flowing down her cheeks and dripping onto the collar of her dress. "I ain't never going to get that blinking silly over someone," she sobbed, "not when it bloody hurts so much when things go . . . bleeding . . . wrong . . ." She dug her fists into her eyes as Mrs. Chubb reached for her.

"There, there, Gertie, luv, don't cry. It'll be all right, you'll see."

Standing awkwardly in the circle of Mrs. Chubb's arms, Gertie struggled to control the awful sobs. After a moment or two she managed to stop, and Mrs. Chubb moved away.

"I'll make you a nice cup of tea," she said, hurrying across to the pantry. "And I'll put some of Michel's best brandy in it. You'll be surprised at how much better you'll feel. You'll be your old self in no time."

Gertie blew her nose on the corner of her apron, convinced that she was never going to be her old self again.

CHAPTER

❊13❊

The minute the front doors of the Pennyfoot opened, Cecily could tell something was wrong. For one thing, Ned barely looked at her as he stepped back to let her in. For another, just a few feet away Baxter paced up and down, hands clasped behind his back and a dark scowl on his face.

As soon as he set eyes on her, he hurried over to her. "Thank God you're back," he muttered. "All hell has broken loose in the ballroom."

Relieved that he wasn't upset about her absence, Cecily slipped out of her coat and handed it to Ned. "Whatever is the matter? What's happened?"

Glancing at Ned, Baxter took hold of Cecily's arm. "You'd better come with me," he said grimly and began leading her down the hallway.

"What is it?" Cecily demanded. "You're beginning to frighten me."

Baxter stopped so suddenly that she bumped into him.

"I beg your pardon, Cecily, that was thoughtless of me."
He pulled himself up straight, the way he always did when
he had bad news to impart.

Watching his face, Cecily braced herself.

"To put matters as simply as possible," Baxter said solemnly, "Phoebe Carter-Holmes has disappeared, and Colonel Fortescue has been arrested."

"I've never heard anything quite so ridiculous in all my
life," Cecily declared as she started off for the ballroom
with Baxter hot on her heels. "What do you mean, Phoebe
has disappeared? What in heaven's name makes the constable believe that the colonel's responsible?"

"She disappeared from the magician's box," Baxter explained as he held the door open for her. "Apparently the
constable caught the colonel in the act."

"In the act of what?" Cecily spotted the policeman—a
man she didn't recognize—seated on his chair in front of
the stage. The colonel sat facing him, his hands tucked
between his knees, and a forlorn expression on his normally
jovial face.

"I'm not really sure," Baxter muttered as Cecily hurried
toward the two men. "To be honest, neither one of them
is making much sense."

Cecily halted in front of the constable, who leapt to his
feet when he saw her.

"Pardon me, mum, but I'm afraid I'll have to ask you
to leave the room," he said, touching the brim of his helmet
with his fingers. "I have secured this here area until the
inspector arrives."

"I am not going anywhere," Cecily said calmly, "until
I learn exactly what has happened here and why you apparently have one of my guests in your custody. This is my
hotel, and I have a right to know what is taking place in
it."

Colonel Fortescue started muttering to himself, shaking
his head and rocking back and forth on his chair.

The constable shifted his feet, beginning to look a little

worried. "Begging your pardon, Mrs. Sinclair. I didn't recognize you. Well, mum, it were like this. I left me post for just a minute or two when . . . ahem . . . nature called, so to speak, and when I returned I found this here gentleman loitering on the stage." He nodded at the colonel. "I saw him open the door of the box and look inside. Then he started talking to himself. When I asked him what he was doing, he told me Mrs. Carter-Holmes had gone."

"Gone? Gone where?"

"Vanished, mum. Disappeared. Vamoosed."

Cecily did her best to curb her irritation. "Constable . . . what is your name?"

"P.C. Shackleston, mum."

"You must be from Wellercombe, Constable Shackleston."

"Yes, mum. I am."

"That is why this understanding has arisen. You obviously are not familiar with the people involved. The colonel tends to get a little confused, but I can assure you he would never harm Mrs. Carter-Holmes. Or anyone else for that matter. I'm quite sure that Mrs. Carter-Holmes most likely has simply gone off somewhere on an errand."

"That's what I thought at first. But the colonel kept insisting that she went into the box and didn't come out. Well, I remembered what happened to the other one what vanished, so I reckoned as how the same thing might have had happened to Mrs. Carter-Holmes. So I told the colonel to sit on a chair until I got back, and I searched all around behind the stage."

"And you didn't find her." In spite of her skepticism, Cecily felt a small pang of apprehension.

"No, mum. I didn't. What's more, when I got back to the colonel, he swore she hadn't come back through the door down there. As far as I could see, there's only two ways out from the stage. Either through that door or down the front steps."

"Yes, that's quite right."

"Well, mum, since the gentleman here couldn't answer my questions to my satisfaction, namely, what he was doing on the stage in the first place, and since the lady seems to be missing, I thought it best to put him under arrest just for the time being."

"I am not responsible for what happened to Phoebe, you blithering idiot!" Fortescue suddenly shouted, jumping to his feet. "By God, man, what are you doing dithering around here when you should be out there looking for the wretched woman?"

"Colonel . . ." Cecily touched his arm.

Fortescue jumped a foot in the air, as if realizing for the first time that she was there. "Oh, there you are, old bean. For God's sake, tell this imbecile here that Phoebe needs help. Those blasted fiends have got her, and if we don't get her back soon, heaven knows what they'll do to her."

"Colonel," Cecily said, as Baxter discreetly moved closer to her side, "please try to tell me exactly what happened."

"What happened? What happened? How the blazes do I know what happened? I watched her walk up onto the stage and go inside that infernal box. She didn't come out again. When I opened the blasted door, she'd gone. *Pouf!*" The colonel snapped his fingers in the air. "Just like that."

Cecily felt a cold chill course down her arms. It couldn't possibly have happened again, could it? "Are you sure Phoebe went inside the box?" she asked, speaking slowly and distinctly.

"Yes, old bean. I saw her open the door with my own eyes and step inside. She was in there so long, I couldn't imagine what she was doing in there, so that's when I toddled over to take a look. I stared right at the blasted thing the whole time. Opened the door and . . ." Fortescue spread his arms out wide. "Nothing. Not a blasted eyelash. Damndest thing I ever saw."

"Mrs. Sinclair," the constable said, sounding apologetic,

"begging your pardon, mum, but I do think the lady might have disappeared just like the other one."

"Of course she disappeared, you numskull! That's what I've been trying to tell you." Fortescue looked as if he were about to explode.

"Steady, old man," Baxter muttered as the policeman held up his hand.

"I suggest you sit down, sir. I wouldn't want to have to cuff you to the chair, but if you don't behave . . ."

"For heaven's sake, man, where are your blasted brains? Can't you see it's those damn blighters who've captured her? Probably waiting to ambush us in the jungle. We'll need a full brigade to go after her, by George. Tell him, Mrs. Sinclair."

"Colonel, perhaps if you calm down a little, we can decide what is best to do."

"We have to go after her, old bean! She's in desperate trouble. Can't let those perishers keep her. They could turn her into a savage in no time."

Cecily stared up at the innocent-looking box on the stage, her mind unable to accept the full significance of what she'd heard. Phoebe couldn't have disappeared. Surely not without the magician's help at the very least.

"You didn't see anyone else near the box?" she asked the colonel, who was strutting back and forth, muttering to himself again.

"Of course not, madam. You can't see the blighters in the dark, anyway. That's why they can get away with everything."

P.C. Shackleston sidled up to Cecily and murmured, "Mrs. Sinclair, I really do think I should lock him up somewhere until the inspector can get here. He could be dangerous, you know."

"It might be as well," Baxter agreed.

Cecily shook her head. "Constable, I can assure you that you have nothing to fear from the colonel. Since you have no proof that he is responsible for Mrs. Carter-Holmes's supposed disappearance, I suggest you wait until we discover what happened to her before you arrest anyone. The inspector doesn't care for mistakes, as I'm sure you know."

At the mention of the inspector the constable looked nervous. "Well," he said doubtfully, "when you put it like that . . ."

"I'll take full responsibility for the colonel's actions," Cecily said recklessly, despite a muffled protest from Baxter. "All he really needs is a stiff brandy, and I'm sure he'll be able to tell us more clearly what actually happened."

"Brandy?" the colonel said, visibly brightening. "I say, old bean, I don't mind if I do. Jolly decent of you, what?"

"Perhaps you'd like to join him, Constable?" Cecily suggested.

Shackleston's face filled with regret. "I don't think I should, mum. Not when I'm on duty, like."

"I don't think anyone will notice." Cecily gave him an encouraging smile. "After all, someone should escort the colonel to the bar, don't you think? That way he can tell you what really happened once he feels better. Just tell the barman that the drinks are on the house."

"Well, that's very kind of you, mum, I'm sure. But I should be watching over this here stage, you see. I can't let anyone go near that box. Especially now that someone else has disappeared."

"Baxter and I will watch over it for you until you come back." She smiled up at Baxter, who was staring at her intently, his gray eyes narrowed in suspicion. "Won't we, Baxter?"

"Well . . ." the constable said doubtfully, "if you're sure, mum . . . I could use a drink. I'm getting cold sitting in this big ballroom. Bit drafty, it is."

"Come on, then, man," the colonel said briskly. "You're wasting time standing here blasted talking about it."

Shackleston nodded. "Very well, but just one little glass, that's all, while you answer my questions properly."

Fortescue looked at him as if he questioned his sanity.

The policeman moved off, and just before the colonel joined him, he leaned close to Cecily and whispered hoarsely, "Send out the brigade to rescue poor old Phoebe. Don't like the thought of her out there all by herself, poor blighter. Someone has to find her."

"We'll find her, Colonel," Cecily promised, trying to sound a great deal more positive than she felt.

She waited until the two men were out of earshot, then said urgently, "Watch the door for me, Baxter. I want to take a closer look at that box."

"I thought as much." Baxter tightened his mouth. "I'd rather you didn't go anywhere near that box."

"I'm only going to look at it."

"And supposing you disappear as well? What am I supposed to do then?"

Cecily raised her eyebrows. "Why, Baxter, pray don't tell me you are beginning to believe in the supernatural, after all your declarations to the contrary?"

Baxter stretched his neck and ran a finger under his collar. "I do not believe in all this talk of evil spirits, of course. I am merely concerned that there is some kind of trap inside the box, and you could very well fall into it. Which is possibly what happened to Mrs. Carter-Holmes."

"Precisely, which is exactly why I must take a closer look."

"But—"

Cecily glanced at the door. "Baxter, I really don't have time to argue. I promise I'll be extremely cautious, and I won't be taken by surprise. But I can't accept the fact that Phoebe simply vanished . . . not on her own, anyway. I must look at that box and now, before the constable returns. I'm quite sure he wouldn't allow me to examine it if I asked him."

"I have to agree with you on that point." Baxter hesitated. "You wouldn't consider keeping watch while I examine the box?"

"I'd rather do it myself, but thank you. I do appreciate the offer."

Baxter sighed. "Very well, but, Cecily . . . do be careful. I don't know what I should do if anything happened to you."

"I'll be careful," Cecily promised. She quickly mounted the steps while Baxter strolled across to the door. Now that she was actually faced with the task, she had to admit she felt a little apprehensive.

Two women had vanished from the contraption, no matter how innocent it appeared. One of them had died. She refused to consider the possibility that Phoebe had shared the same grisly fate.

She approached the box warily, not quite sure what to expect. The constable must have closed the door again, as it was tightly shut.

Hoping fervently that it wasn't locked, Cecily grasped the handle and turned. The door swung open on silent hinges, revealing the dark, empty space within, waiting expectantly for her to enter.

Shaking off her fanciful fears, Cecily stepped inside. She half closed the door behind her but left it open enough to shed some light into the narrow compartment.

The box smelled faintly of rose water and the musty odor of damp cedar. As far as Cecily could see, it was an ordinary, plain box with bare walls and floor. The only adornment in the entire structure was a carved rose, mounted on the back wall.

Cecily stared at it, wondering where she had recently heard someone mention a rose. After a moment it came to her. Charlotte's last remark just before she left had struck Cecily as a little odd coming from someone as coarse as the magician's wife. What was it she'd said? *Like they say, not every rose smells as sweet as it looks.*

Cecily felt a twinge of excitement. Charlotte had been talking about illusions not being what they seemed. Had she unwittingly revealed a clue to the secret of the box?

There was only one way to find out. Nervously holding her breath, Cecily reached for the rose. At first there was no reaction from her probing fingers, but then she pushed a little harder. From a corner of the box she heard a soft click.

To her amazement the wall seemed to be disintegrating in front of her. For a moment she almost panicked, poised to flee from her eerie confinement, but then she realized that the wall was actually a folding partition, sliding back to reveal a narrow cavity behind it.

No one except an extremely thin person could possibly squeeze herself into the cramped space. But Denmarric's assistants had all been painfully thin. Reaching across the space, Cecily found a latch. She lifted it, and the back of the box swung open onto the wings.

Now she knew how the trick was done. Denmarric had put Ivy into what had appeared to the audience to be an empty box and had then closed the door.

As soon as she was hidden from the audience, Ivy had unfolded the partition, stepped behind it, and closed it again.

When Denmarric opened the door of the box again, all the audience saw was the same box they'd seen before; only now Ivy was hidden behind the partition.

Denmarric then wheeled the box over to the wings, saying he would make Ivy reappear in the second box, which stood in front of the curtains.

Once the first box was positioned, Ivy would then leave through the rear door, run through the wings backstage to the curtains, slip through while Denmarric had the attention of the audience, and enter through the rear of the second box. Denmarric would then throw open the door, and Ivy would have miraculously been transferred from one box to another.

Except that this time, someone encountered Ivy after she left the first box. The big question, of course, was who had wanted to be rid of Ivy badly enough to kill her.

A loud bout of coughing interrupted her thoughts, and Cecily started. That was Baxter's signal that the constable was returning. Remaining inside the box, she carefully closed the front door, then stepped across the hidden compartment to the rear. She closed both the partition and the rear door behind her as she stepped into the wings. Denmarric's secret was safe, at least for the time being.

Her discovery, however, had raised an even more important question, Cecily thought as she hurried through the wings to the ballroom door. Now that Denmarric's amazing vanishing act had proved to be a perfectly logical process, it put a sinister turn to the colonel's story.

If Phoebe had disappeared, it was certainly not by any magical means. Someone had apparently detained Ivy while she was en route to the second box. Had that same person encountered Phoebe stepping out of the box? If so, he might have deemed it necessary to silence the witness in order to escape detection. Phoebe's life could very well be in mortal danger.

CHAPTER

❧ 14 ❧

Cecily reached the door of the ballroom and carefully opened it. Baxter stood talking to the policeman, who had his back to her. Baxter's eyes widened for an instant as he caught sight of her; then he hastily averted his gaze.

Cecily slipped through the door and closed it behind her. "I've examined the pillars as you suggested, Baxter," she called out as she approached, "and they do seem to be in need of repair. I shall see to it at once."

The constable swung around to face her. "Oh, there you are, Mrs. Sinclair," he exclaimed. "I was just asking Mr. Baxter where you were. I didn't see you when I came in."

Baxter's face signaled relief and amazement as he stared at her.

Cecily gave him a slight shake of her head, then smiled at the constable. "I must have been behind one of the pillars. One has to keep such a close watch on these things.

The slightest crack could easily weaken the structure if not taken care of at once.''

''Indeed it could, mum. Speaking of which, I think I should tell you I'm not at all sure about that colonel chap. I left him in the bar knocking back another gin, but I don't think it's going to make him think more clearly. Quite the opposite, if I may say so. Now there's someone who's cracked if I ever saw one.''

''Oh, dear,'' Cecily murmured. ''Well, perhaps I can make some sense of what he says. One has to know how to handle Colonel Fortescue, you know. Just leave him to me, Constable.''

''Yes, mum.'' The constable cleared his throat. ''There's still the matter of Mrs. Carter-Holmes, I'm afraid. The inspector's on his way, and I'm quite sure he'll want to question the old gentleman. He's not as patient as I am, mum, if you know what I mean. I think it might be a good idea to see that the colonel sobers up before he gets here.''

''You're probably right.'' Cecily frowned. ''I'll have a word with him right away.''

She caught Baxter staring at her, as if he couldn't quite believe his eyes. ''Baxter,'' she said gently, ''perhaps you would accompany me while I talk to the colonel?''

He nodded as if in a daze but followed her from the ballroom without a word. Once outside in the hallway, however, he turned on her and muttered, ''How the blazes did you manage that?''

''Manage what?''

''That . . . that . . . you know what I mean.''

''Ah . . . you mean my trick of being in two places at once.''

Rather enjoying his bewilderment, she had a small taste of how it must feel to baffle an audience with illusion.

''That's exactly what I mean. How did you do it?''

She told him and was quite gratified when he complimented her on her astute observation. ''I'm very worried about Phoebe, though," she said as they approached the bar.

"At least that explains how Mrs. Carter-Holmes managed to disappear before Fortescue's eyes."

"It doesn't tell us where she disappeared to or who killed Ivy. I'm very much afraid that Phoebe could be in the murderer's hands."

Baxter paused at the door of the bar. "I sincerely hope that you are mistaken."

Cecily looked up at him, grateful for his concern. "So do I," she said quietly.

The colonel sat at a corner table by himself, much to Cecily's relief. He got unsteadily to his feet as she and Baxter approached. "Did you send out the blasted brigade?" he asked anxiously.

"Not yet, Colonel." Cecily eyed his empty glass. "May we join you for a moment?"

"Of course, old bean. You, too, old chap." The colonel peered at Baxter. "What'll you have, old boy?"

"Nothing, thank you, Colonel," Baxter said with a visible shudder. "Too early in the day for me, I'm afraid."

"Never too early, old boy. You'll have one, won't you, Mrs. Sinclair?"

Cecily shook her head. "Thank you, no, Colonel. But I would like to ask you a question or two." She sat down on the chair Baxter pulled out for her and waited for her manager to seat himself.

Fortescue slumped down on his chair and looked gloomily at his glass. "Went down dashed fast, that one did. Almost forgotten what it tasted like."

"If you would just answer my questions, Colonel, I'll see that your glass is refilled," Cecily promised, ignoring Baxter's sharp look of reproof.

"Oh, jolly decent of you, old girl. Much appreciated, I'm sure."

"Colonel, I want you to try to remember every word Phoebe said to you before she went inside the box."

Fortescue shook his head. "Not a word, madam. She simply opened the door, stepped inside, and shut the blasted door behind her."

"And you waited how long for her to come out again?"

The colonel started blinking furiously. "Not sure I remember that, old bean. Sort of fuzzy, you might say. It seemed like a dashed long time. I kept thinking that constable chappie was coming back, and I was worried dear old Phoebe would get into trouble, you see."

Cecily exchanged a glance with Baxter, wondering since when her friend had become so dear to the colonel. "So you went up onto the stage to find out what happened to Phoebe?"

The colonel snapped his fingers. "That's it! Now I remember. I waited and waited, and when she didn't come out, I went to get her. Thought the door might be stuck. Some of them don't always open from the inside, you know."

"I see. And when you opened the door?"

"Gone. Just like that. Nothing inside the box but air. All that was left of Phoebe was her smell." He leaned forward and whispered hoarsely, "She smells like roses, you know."

Cecily nodded. "And what happened after that?"

"Well, I just stood there, flabbergasted, trying to think what had happened to her, and that dashed policeman came up behind me and demanded to know what I was doing."

"And neither of you saw Phoebe after that?"

"Not a glimmer, old bean. I'm jolly sure I would have seen her come through the door, but she didn't. I can swear to it. And the constable couldn't find her when he looked behind the stage. She just disappeared, like that Deirdre person the other night." The colonel's face suddenly crumpled, and he looked as if he were about to cry.

"Don't worry, Colonel," Cecily said, getting to her feet. "We'll find her."

"I just hope that blasted black beast isn't sitting over her grave, that's all."

His words chilled her, and she was about to reassure him when she remembered something. "Colonel, when you talked about the dog earlier, you mentioned that it bore the mark of the Lord on its forehead. Can you describe that mark?"

Fortescue shook his head in his usual befuddled way. "A cross, I think. A broken cross. Can't remember exactly, old bean."

She ordered another brandy for him and left him staring moodily into the glass. Baxter followed her out of the bar, then fell in step beside her as she hurried down the hall.

"The colonel seems quite devastated by all this," he commented as Cecily paused at the foot of the stairs.

"He does indeed. I feel quite certain now that Phoebe did not leave this hotel under her own free will. If she did uncover the secret of the box, she would surely not have left here without telling someone what she had discovered."

"Perhaps she felt that the illusion should be kept a secret, to protect Denmarric's reputation."

"Perhaps. On the other hand, Phoebe is as anxious as I am to have this matter cleared up in order to avoid canceling the presentation. I'm quite sure she would at least have left a message for me, since I mentioned that the murder would be impossible to solve until we knew exactly how Ivy had disappeared."

"Then you believe she is in the hands of Ivy's murderer?"

Cecily looked up at him. "Yes, Baxter, I do. I'm convinced she has been abducted."

"What was all that talk about the dog?"

"I'm not sure." Cecily frowned. "I do believe I know who owns the dog that the colonel saw sitting by the side of Ivy's grave. I saw a dog like that when I went to see George Dalrymple."

"You think he's involved in Ivy's murder?"

"I don't know, Baxter. At the moment I'm more concerned about what has happened to Phoebe. But I can assure you, if she has been harmed in any way, George Dalrymple will have some difficult questions to answer."

An hour later, the inspector arrived. Cecily met him in the library, and his face was grave as he greeted her.

"I have to tell you, Mrs. Sinclair, that I'm afraid we may very well find another dead body in the woods tomorrow. I must confess I don't know how the crime was perpetrated, but there is no doubt in my mind that whatever happened to Miss Glumm has also befallen Mrs. Carter-Holmes. I intend to launch a search for her, but I am not optimistic as to the outcome."

"Thank you, Inspector. I appreciate your efforts."

"I have sent a messenger to inform the Reverend Carter-Holmes that his mother is missing," Inspector Cranshaw went on. "I am also taking Colonel Fortescue down to the station for further questioning, since he was the last person to see the victim alive."

Cecily bit back a cry of protest. She was not about to concede to the assumption of Phoebe's death until she was presented with the evidence of such. Her heart ached with worry, but she decided not to reveal what she had learned about the box just yet. Nothing could be gained without further investigation, and she wanted nothing to delay the efforts of the inspector and his men to conduct the search.

After Cranshaw had left, she hurried down to Baxter's office. She found him sitting at his desk with his head buried in his hands. He rose at once as she entered.

"Are you ill?" she asked in quick concern.

He smiled wearily at her. "No, my dear madam. Just deeply worried."

"About Phoebe? That's what I came to talk to you about. I think we should arrange our own search party to look for her. While I'm sure the inspector will arrange an adequate search, I would feel much better if we had extra people out there to assist us.''

Baxter nodded. "Very well. But my concern was mostly for you. Now that you know the secret of the box, your life could very well be in danger as well.''

"Ah, but nobody knows that I've learned the secret.''

"And I sincerely hope and trust that you will not reveal that fact to any of your suspects in the hope of forcing them to reveal their guilt.''

Cecily opened her eyes wide. "I would hope I would not be that foolish.''

Baxter narrowed his eyes. "One can always live in hope, I suppose.''

She leaned over and patted his hand. "Come, Baxter, we have more important things to worry about now. I'm anxious to start the search.''

"Nothing is more important to me than your welfare, Cecily.'' Baxter grasped her hand and raised it to his lips.

"Nor yours to me.'' She smiled fondly at him. "I promise I shall take care.''

Baxter heaved a heavy sigh. "I suppose I shall have to be content with that.''

Algie stared at the policeman, refusing to believe what he had just heard. "My m-m-m-m-mother missing? I . . . ah . . . don't understand. How can she . . . ah . . . disappear from a b-b-b-b-box? What was she . . . ah . . . d-d-d-doing in a b-box . . . i-i-i-in the first place?''

The constable shrugged, not too sympathetically, Algie thought, trying to fight off an overwhelming feeling of panic in his chest.

"All I can tell you, sir, is that your mother disappeared from a box belonging to the Great Denmarric. The lads say she was spirited away, just like Ivy Glumm.''

"S-s-s-spirited away? "B-b-b-y whom?''

The constable gave him a pitying look. "The evil spirits, Vicar.''

"Evil spirits!" The thought outraged Algie. Making a tremendous effort to control his stutter, he said carefully, "Constable, I must remind you that you are in God's house. I can assure you, the only spirit c-capable of taking my mother dwells in the Lord, and I am quite sure he would n-n-not have taken her b-body away without a decent burial."

"Yes, sir. I mean no, sir."

Algie clasped his hands together to stop them from shaking.

"What is Inspector Cranshaw d-d-d-oing about this?"

"He has launched a search for Mrs. Carter-Holmes, Vicar. They are searching the woods where Ivy's body was found."

Algie uttered a soft moan. This couldn't be happening. Not to his own mother. Nevertheless, she had to be found, whether or not she was still in possession of her soul. "Very well," he muttered brokenly. "P-p-please inform me at once if you f-f-find her."

"Of course we will, Vicar. I'm sorry, sir." The constable turned smartly and clomped up the aisle, the heels of his boots ringing out on the wooden floor.

Algie slumped against the pulpit, his head hazy with incoherent thoughts. Thank heavens choir practice was over, and he was alone. It was easier to think when he was alone.

He had last seen his mother that morning. She had talked about visiting Mrs. Sinclair at the Pennyfoot Hotel. He had gone to the church soon after she'd left, and he'd been there ever since.

He had heard the talk about Ivy Glumm's body being found in the woods but hadn't paid too much attention. Now that he really thought about it, he remembered his mother mentioning something about a magic act that had gone wrong, sending that poor unfortunate girl to her demise.

Algie moaned again. His mother was always poking her nose into things that didn't concern her. How many times had he warned her that one day her inquisitive nature would lead her into trouble? And now it seemed as if his fears had been well justified.

He could not imagine how she had become involved with a magician in the first place, however. He had strongly objected when she'd first announced that she had hired one for a presentation at the Pennyfoot.

As usual, his mother had haughtily dismissed his objections as outmoded and unimaginative. She had charged forward in her usual forthright way and was now paying a heavy price for her obstinacy.

Algie shook his head in despair. What to do? What to do? He couldn't just stand around and wait for someone to tell him what was happening. He had to do something.

He turned and stared up at the figure of Christ behind the alter. His lips moving in prayer, he walked slowly forward, then sank onto his knees.

The answer came to him, as clearly as a spoken word. He must join in the search. Immediately. But not alone. He must enlist help. There was only one group of people he could think of who could be gathered together in a comparatively short time. His mother's dance troupe.

He would round them up, he decided as he stumbled to his feet, and together they would search the entire village. God willing, they would find his mother alive and well.

CHAPTER

❁15❁

Cecily looked around the members of the staff crowded into the library, touched by their willingness to help search for her friend. Baxter had asked for volunteers, and no one had refused him.

He stood with his back to the fireplace, dividing the silent people into small groups and designating areas of the village for them to search. As usual, he was meticulous and commanding, and she felt a flush of pride as she watched him issue his quiet but direct orders.

"The vicarage shall be our headquarters," he announced when everyone understood their instructions. "If Mrs. Carter-Holmes is found, she will be brought back there. If you should lose contact with the rest of the party, or if you feel too weary to continue, report back to the vicarage so that we know everyone is accounted for. Are there any questions?"

There was a general shaking of heads and murmurs of assurance.

"Very good. Samuel will have the traps ready for those who will go to the farthest end of the village. The rest of you will search on foot. All that is left to say now is that Mrs. Sinclair and I greatly appreciate your efforts, and we pray that Mrs. Carter-Holmes will be found safe and well."

The staff members began filing out, one by one, their faces showing their concern. Mrs. Chubb paused in front of Cecily, fighting back tears. "We'll find her, won't we, mum?" she whispered.

"I'm sure we shall," Cecily assured her. "Phoebe is very good at taking care of herself."

Mrs. Chubb nodded, though she didn't look too convinced. "I'll be staying here to take care of Gertie's babies while she and the girls join the search," she said, pausing to blow her nose on a large white handkerchief. "I'd just like to say that my heart will be with you all. I pray that you find her before . . . before . . . ."

"Try not to worry, Mrs. Chubb." Cecily patted her shoulder. "We don't want to upset the babies, now, do we?"

"No, mum, quite right." Mrs. Chubb tucked her handkerchief away in her sleeve and squared her plump shoulders. "If I might just make a suggestion, mum? It might be a good idea to ask for Miss Pengrath's help, seeing as how she sees things what the rest of us don't."

"A very good suggestion," Cecily agreed, though she had already had the same thought herself.

"There's something else I have to tell you, mum, though I reckon it can wait until all this worry is over. I best be off now. Gertie will be wanting me down there taking care of her babies."

Cecily watched her housekeeper hurry out of the door, wondering what it was Mrs. Chubb had to tell her. Not more bad news, she hoped fervently. She didn't think she could face any more misfortunes.

Baxter closed the door behind the last volunteer and walked over to where she stood by the French windows. "Are you sure you want to join in the search?" he asked gently. "You look exhausted."

She smiled weakly at him. "More worried than weary, I assure you. I couldn't bear the thought of waiting here for word. I'd much rather be with you."

"Very well. I'll help Samuel with the traps, and you can meet me at the front steps. We'll go directly to Miss Pengrath's house, then out to Parson's Peak."

"I'll be there just as soon as I've collected my hat and coat."

He held her to him for an instant, saying gruffly, "I'm sorry, Cecily. I know how difficult this is for you. I wish I could spare you any more grief."

His words only deepened her anxiety. She knew what was in his mind. Phoebe had been missing for several hours. Even if they found her, it was unlikely they would find her alive. The thought that her dear friend had walked into danger right there in the hotel was almost more than Cecily could bear. That knowledge would torment her for the rest of her days.

Algie surveyed the bedraggled group of dancers shivering in the bright moonlight on the lawn in front of the church. They didn't look capable of locating their own noses, leave alone his missing mother.

Nevertheless, they were all he had right now, and he was determined to make the best of a bad situation. "The p-p-police are searching the woods," he announced, silently cursing his wayward tongue. "So I suggest we s-s-s-search the fields behind the George and Dragon."

"Brilliant idea," a dry voice answered. "That way we can knock back a stiff brandy or two when we get cold."

"Shut up, Marion," someone else muttered. "You know what happens to you when you drink."

"Yeah, she pees in her drawers," another girl answered,

nudging her companion so hard she almost fell over.

"I'll bleeding sock you in the kisser," Marion threatened, raising her fist.

"Ladies, please," Algie whined, wishing his mother was there to control the unruly assemblage. But then, had she been there, none of this would have been necessary. "Must I remind you that my mother's very life is in danger? We must all work together to find her as s-s-soon as possible."

"He's right, Marion," a tall, skinny girl said sharply. "Mrs. Carter-Holmes could be dead, just like that Ivy Glumm. So stop your larking about, and let's get on with it."

Gazing gratefully at Belinda, the girl who had spoken, Algie took up his position at the head of the group. "J-j-just follow me until I give the word to spread out."

"We follow him and we're likely to end up in the bleeding ocean," someone muttered.

"Shut *up!*" someone else snapped.

"I think we should sing while we march," Dora piped up. "Like they do in the army."

"How'd you know what they bleeding do in the army?" Marion rudely demanded.

"My dad told me, so there."

"They wouldn't have your dad in the bleeding Boy Scouts, leave alone the army."

"You take that back, Marion, or I'll—"

Algie closed his mind to the squabbling behind him. Maybe it was a mistake to enlist the aid of such a high-spirited, unreliable group of misfits, but it was too late to do anything about it now.

At the very least, they were extra eyes, and something told him that if his mother was going to be found, he was going to need all the help he could get.

Madeline received the news of Phoebe's disappearance with a calm assurance that went a long way toward easing Cecily's mind. Mindful of keeping the secret of the box to

herself for the time being, Cecily told Madeline only that
Phoebe had apparently disappeared the same way that Ivy
Glumm vanished from the stage that night.

Madeline asked for a few moments alone and disappeared through her bead curtains while Baxter and Cecily
waited in the cluttered living room.

Cecily could tell from Baxter's expression that he was
skeptical of anything Madeline might tell them, but Cecily
knew her friend well enough to know that at times Madeline could be surprisingly accurate with her predictions.

Baxter said nothing as they waited but stood by the door,
his hands clasped behind his back, as if anxious to be on
his way.

After a short while Madeline returned. She had thrown
a shawl over her shoulders and had tied a silk scarf over
her limp straw hat. "I've decided to join you in the
search," she announced.

Baxter stepped forward to offer his hand as Cecily struggled to rise. "You know where she is?" she asked eagerly.

To her intense disappointment, Madeline shook her head.
"The location eludes me. But I can tell you that Phoebe is
alive. I would certainly know if she were not."

Feeling somewhat frustrated, Cecily had to accept that.
"Come, then," she said. "We shall begin our search of
Parson's Peak. I can only hope that the skies will remain
clear in order to give us the benefit of moonlight."

"That I can promise you." Madeline moved to the door,
but Baxter reached it first and pulled it open for her. Instead
of stepping outside, however, she turned in the doorway.
"Cecily, I know I am choosing an unfortunate time to mention this, but I feel I should discuss the matter with you
now."

Looking at Madeline's grave face, Cecily felt chilled.
"What is it, Madeline?"

"Have you spoken to Ethel today?"

Surprised at the question, Cecily shook her head. "No,
I haven't. Now that you mention it, I don't remember see-

ing Ethel at the staff meeting in the library this evening.''
She brought her hand to her throat. ''Oh, please don't tell
me she has disappeared as well.''

''Not as far as I know.'' Madeline came back into the
room. ''Cecily, I'm sorry to be the one to tell you this, but
Ethel is very ill. I thought you should know at once, in
view of the fact that she is contagious. I had intended telling
you tomorrow, but since you are here . . .''

Cecily's cry of dismay echoed Baxter's muffled exclamation. ''Oh, that poor child. I've been concerned that her
cough might be serious. I've been meaning to talk to her
about it myself, but with everything else that has been happening around here lately, it slipped my mind. Has Dr.
Prestwick been informed?''

Madeline sighed. ''I believe she was going today.''

''So that is what Mrs. Chubb intended to tell me,'' Cecily murmured. ''This is grave news. Ethel will no doubt
have to go to a sanitarium. We shall miss her.''

Madeline pulled her shawl closer around her shoulders.
''I haven't said anything to Ethel yet, but after her treatment, I would like to offer my home for her recuperation.
I have the knowledge and the means to take care of her. If
her treatment is successful, it will simply be a matter of
seeing that she has rest, good food, and peace of mind.''

Cecily gazed at her friend, momentarily speechless.
When she found her voice, she said unsteadily, ''That could
take a very long time, Madeline. Years, perhaps.''

''I'm aware of that. But I feel that she will fare better
with someone to take care of her needs, and she will be
close enough for her husband and friends to visit often.''

''You are a good woman, Madeline Pengrath,'' Baxter
said as Cecily tried to find words to express her feelings.
''Such generosity will surely be repaid.''

''My payment will come in watching Ethel's good health
restored to her.'' Madeline turned back to the door. ''Now
let us see if we can find where Phoebe is hiding herself.''

•   •   •

"We can't bleeding go in there," Gertie exclaimed in a hoarse whisper. "Them blinking woods belong to Lord Withersgill. His bloody gamekeeper will shoot us for bleeding trespassing."

"Not if we explain why we're there." Samuel threw his leg across the stile. "Besides, who's going to see us in the dark?"

"I don't want to go in there and get shot at," Doris said, her voice wavering.

"Don't be such a baby, Doris." Daisy hitched up her skirt and hopped over the stile to join Samuel. "Samuel's right, no one will see us. Look how dark it is. It must be past midnight by now. They'll all be asleep."

"I'm tired." Doris sat down on the bottom rung of the stile. "I can't go no farther. We've been searching for hours."

"I reckon the old girl's dead by now, anyhow," Samuel said, peering into the darkness surrounding the woods. "Them spirits have done away with her, you mark my words."

"Shut up about bleeding spirits, Samuel Rawlins," Gertie snapped. "You'll frighten the girls."

"Frighten you, you mean." Samuel lifted his hands and wagged his fingers, uttering a low moan. His face looked eerie and somehow evil in the pale shadows cast by the moon.

Gertie felt as if someone were running cold fingers down the back of her neck. She heard Doris whimper and in her fright lashed out at Samuel. "Stop it!" she yelled. "Shut your silly, bleeding face, Samuel."

"Listen," Daisy said in a low urgent voice that made Gertie even more nervous.

They all fell quiet, and for a moment all Gertie could hear was the rustling of leaves in the wind and the splashing of a nearby brook. Then she heard what Daisy's keen ears had apparently heard. The faint thundering of hoofbeats.

"The gamekeeper," Doris whispered, scrabbling up onto the stile.

"I'll tell him we're looking for Mrs. Carter-Holmes," Samuel said, sounding defiant.

"What got taken away by bleeding evil spirits." Gertie gave Doris a shove that sent her stumbling over the stile. "Who's bloody going to believe that bleeding nonsense?"

"You believed it," Samuel reminded her. "That's why we're all out here looking for her."

"That doesn't mean I believe in evil spirits." Gertie felt a little more secure now that she was standing on the other side of the stile. "You'd better blinking well get over here, both of you. That gamekeeper's getting bleeding close, and he's just as bleeding likely to shoot at you than stop to ask flipping questions."

"We ain't done nothing wrong," Samuel protested, but Daisy was already scrambling over the stile.

At least, she started to, but then her foot got caught and she fell back, landing heavily on the ground. Her startled yelp carried easily across the silent field.

The rider reined in, paused, then turned in their direction. "Get up, Daisy!" Gertie said urgently. "He's bleeding seen us."

Samuel grabbed Daisy's arm and hauled her to her feet. By now the ground shook with the thundering of hooves.

Daisy threw a desperate look over her shoulder, then uttered a cry of dismay. "It's not the gamekeeper. It's Lord Withersgill hisself."

"Strewth," Gertie muttered. "We're bleeding well in for it now."

"I wish we hadn't come," Marion complained as she trudged along the narrow path across the moonlit field several yards behind the vicar. "I'm cold and tired, and after all that looking, we never found his flipping mother."

"He's really upset about it, too," Dora said, keeping her voice low so that Algie couldn't hear her. "I don't blame him. It must be awful to have your mother stolen away by evil spirits. You never know what really happened to her, do you?''

''We all know what happened to Ivy Glumm,'' Marion said, slapping her upper arms to get warm. ''She got buried alive, that's what. They say the spirits waited until she went to sleep, then put her in a hole and covered her up with dirt so's she couldn't breathe no more.''

''Ee-yew.'' Dora shuddered, while the rest of the girls uttered sounds of disgust.

''Just imagine waking up and finding all that dirt going up your nose and in your mouth,'' Marion said, beginning to enjoy the sensation she was causing.

The cries from the other girls intensified.

''Shut up, Marion,'' Dora warned. ''You'll make us all sick.''

Marion tossed her head. ''That shouldn't take much. You only have to look in the mirror. Better be careful, though. You might see the evil spirits what took Ivy away.''

''Well, I don't believe no evil spirits took Ivy nor Mrs. Carter-Holmes away, so there,'' Dora said. ''There's no such things as evil spirits. I think Ivy met someone in the woods who done her in. There's lots of strange people walking around in the woods at night. It could have been one of them gypsies.''

Secretly Marion was rather glad to hear that. She would much sooner deal with flesh-and-blood villains than spiritual ones. She was reluctant, though, to let go of her momentary glory. She liked frightening the others. It gave her a feeling of power.

Just at that moment she spotted a shadowy figure standing alone in the middle of the field. Grasping the opportunity to exploit her advantage one last time, she pointed a shaky finger at the dark silhouette. ''Oo, look,'' she said, making her voice all shivery, ''there's an evil spirit right there.''

Several of the girls started shrieking, hanging on to each

other for grim death. Marion stuffed her fist in her mouth to stop from laughing as Algie charged back down the path toward them.

"What is it? Have you found her? Is she all right?"

"Evil spirits," one of the girls shrieked, amid a chorus of shrill screams.

Algie peered shortsightedly across the field. Even from there, in the shadowy moonlight he could see quite plainly what it was. "That's just a scarecrow, you silly girls."

The screams died down, and the girls huddled together, looking forlorn.

"We're all t-tired," Algie said on a note of defeat. "I think it's time we went back to the vicarage."

"About time," Marion muttered.

"I'm sorry, Vicar," Belinda said, touching Algie's sleeve. "I wish we could have found her."

Algie felt his throat begin to close, and he had to wait a moment before he could answer. "Yes, well, thank you. All of you. Let us hope that someone else has found my mother by now and that she's safe and sound at the vicarage. If not, I really don't know what I shall do."

Even Marion didn't have an answer to that.

CHAPTER

❁ 16 ❁

"She isn't here," Madeline said.

Cecily paused and looked at her friend. The wind had picked up during the last hour, a damp, cold wind from the sea that seemed to penetrate her very bones.

Madeline seemed unaffected by the cold, with only her light shawl to keep the chill from her slender body. She stood quite still in the moonlight, her hair drifting about her shoulders, her face a pale shadow against the backdrop of the bright starlit sky.

"Are you sure?" Cecily passed a weary hand across her eyes. She couldn't remember ever feeling quite so tired.

"Quite sure. We are looking in the wrong place."

Baxter, who had marched on ahead, strode rapidly back to where they stood. "Is something wrong?" He peered at Cecily, his expression hidden by the shadows. "Are you hurt?"

Cecily shook her head. "Just . . . very tired. Madeline

seems to think we are searching in the wrong place.''

"Listen." Madeline lifted her chin and stared intently in the direction of the village.

From the valley below Cecily heard the faint baying of dogs. She shivered, still unable to accept the fact that Phoebe could be out in this dark night, all alone, maybe hurt . . . or even . . .

She wouldn't allow herself to think negative thoughts. Wherever Phoebe was, she was in charge of the situation as always. She had to believe that, Cecily told herself.

"They've brought out the dogs," Baxter said, sounding immeasurably weary. "That must mean they still haven't found her."

"I think we should go back to the vicarage." Madeline spoke with such conviction in her voice that both Cecily and Baxter stared at her.

"But we haven't finished searching up here yet." Cecily swept out her arm. "We haven't even looked in those trees over there."

"We're in the wrong place." The end of Madeline's shawl wafted in the breeze, and she snatched it back. "We'll go to the vicarage. That's where we'll find her. I'm sure of it."

Cecily felt a leap of hope. "You mean you think someone else has found her already?"

"I can't tell. I don't think so." Madeline started off down the path, her feet crunching lightly on the pebbles.

Cecily stared after her for a minute or two, then looked at Baxter. "I'm not sure I understand."

Baxter tucked his hands into the pockets of his coat. "I'm inclined to treat her statements with a great degree of skepticism."

"But there could be a chance that she's right."

He shrugged. "In that case I shall be the first to congratulate her. In any case, you are too tired to continue this search tonight. I suggest we all go back to the vicarage and report to whoever is there. Then we shall go home."

There was nothing more that Cecily would like better than to go home. She wasn't at all sure, however, how well she'd sleep if Phoebe hadn't been found.

Doris stared in fascination as Lord Withersgill reined in his magnificent black horse and came to a prancing stop in front of them. She'd never been this close to the squire before, but she'd heard plenty about him from Daisy.

Lord Withersgill had once rescued her sister from certain death, when she fell over the cliffs on Putney Downs and spent the night on a narrow ledge no bigger than a fireside hearth.

Daisy had gone on for weeks about how handsome and brave was the new lord of the manor until Doris had been sick of hearing his name.

Looking at him now, though, astride his restless horse in the full glow of the moonlight, his handsome face half shadowed by the brim of his top hat, he looked mysterious and terribly exciting. Doris could quite well see how Daisy would get mushy over him.

Actually, Daisy seemed to have lost her wits at that moment. She stood gazing up at Lord Withersgill as if she'd never seen a man on a horse before. Gertie looked just as dumbstruck, staring down at her feet with her face all red. At least Samuel had the presence of mind to snatch off his cap.

"Isn't it a little late for a picnic?" Lord Withersgill inquired in a voice so deep and pleasant Doris could feel the effects of it all the way down to her toes.

Everyone turned to look at Samuel, who stood shuffling his feet as if he'd forgotten how to talk. Losing patience with him, Doris burst out,"We're looking for Mrs. Carter-Holmes."

Her heart did a little dance when the squire's dark eyes looked her way. He stared at her for a moment, then turned his gaze back to Daisy. "Good Lord," he muttered. "There are two of them."

Determined to hold his attention now that she had it, Doris leaned over the stile, the way she'd seen the women in magazine pictures do, and gave him her most becoming smile. "I'm Doris, your lordship, and she's Daisy. She's the one what you rescued last summer. We're twins, and I'm a singer."

Daisy recovered her senses and glared at Doris with a look that clearly warned her to shut up.

Lord Withersgill looked amused. "Really. And what does all this have to do with Mrs. Carter-Holmes?"

Samuel cleared his throat. "She's missing, your lordship. Disappeared this afternoon. Half the village is out looking for her."

Lord Withersgill's smile vanished. "I see. Where was the lady last seen?"

Samuel cleared his throat again. "Well, it were like this. Mrs. Carter-Holmes went inside a box belonging to the Great Denmarric, and she never came out again."

Astonishment washed over the squire's face. "You are talking about Mrs. Carter-Holmes, the vicar's mother?"

"Yes, sir. I mean, your lordship."

"I thought it was someone called Ivy Glumm who disappeared from the stage that night."

"Yes, sir, it were. But now Mrs. Carter-Holmes has gone and vanished, too."

"Good Lord." The squire tipped his hat back, allowing the moon to fall full on his face.

Doris thought she was going to swoon at the beauty of him. She'd never seen such a handsome man in her entire life.

"I suppose the constabulary has been informed?" Lord Withersgill's horse sidestepped with impatience, but the squire controlled the powerful animal with a flick of the reins.

"Yes, your lordship. They are searching the woods on Putney Downs. We was sent up here to look. I didn't realize we was trespassing on your land, sir. I apologize."

Doris glared at him. Blinking liar. He knew quite well it were the lord's lands.

"That's quite all right, lad. Keep looking all you want. I'll get back to the manor and alert my staff." The lord turned his horse's head, then paused to look down into Daisy's face. "I trust you recovered from your ghastly ordeal last summer?"

Daisy dropped a deep curtsey. "Oh, yes, your lordship. Thank you kindly. I shall never forget your bravery."

Lord Withersgill laughed—a rich, full sound that turned Doris's knees to water. "I am most happy to have been of assistance. It is always an honor indeed to rescue a lady in distress. Good night to you all. Or should I say good morning? I wish you success in finding Mrs. Carter-Holmes alive and well."

With a friendly wave of his hand he cantered off up the hill, while the little group by the stile watched him in awed silence.

Doris was the first one to break the spell. "Oo, my," she said with a sigh. "Now there goes a real toff if I ever saw one."

Daisy clambered over the stile, a silly smile plastered all over her face. "He called me a lady," she said, her voice all soft and mawkish. "Did you hear him? He called me a lady in distress."

Put out that she wasn't the one being so honored, Doris said sharply, "He was just being polite. Toffs talk like that all the time."

"How would you know?" demanded Samuel. "You ain't exactly an expert on toffs, having never met any."

"I've met plenty of toffs," Doris said hotly. "I've been waiting on enough of them in the hotel. None of them what looked like that, though, that I will say."

Samuel snorted. "Well, you can take that silly look off your face. Toffs like him don't look at housemaids. Not unless they want a bit of fun, like."

"Don't talk about him that way," Daisy said, shoving

Samuel's shoulder. "Lord Withersgill's not that sort."

"Ouch!" Samuel rubbed his shoulder. "How'd you know, anyhow?"

"I know," Daisy said with quiet conviction. "He's a proper gentleman, our lord of the manor, and I won't have no one say as he isn't."

"Well, anyway, Sam Rawlins," Doris put in, "I bet if I was a famous singer he'd look at me. Just wait until I'm as famous as Bella DelRay. I'll have toffs like him lining up at the stage door just panting to look at me, so there."

"Them kind of bloody toffs I wouldn't give you bleeding tuppence for," Gertie said, turning her nose up in the air. "They're not bleeding gentlemen like Lord Withersgill. They're just out for what they can bloody get, and if they don't get it, they'll flipping look for it somewhere else."

"Yeah, look at Bella DelRay," Samuel put in. "She's been a famous singer for a long time, and she don't have no one, does she? She lives all alone in a big house. That's why she wants you to go and live with her, 'cos she's lonely."

"You wouldn't want to be bleeding lonely in a big city like London," Gertie said, wagging a finger at Doris. "It's dangerous for women who are lonely and don't know no one."

"I'll know Bella DelRay." Doris lifted her chin, determined not to let them all see how much they were scaring her.

Gertie laughed. "Don't be bleeding daft. She ain't going to do you no good, is she? She's going to be off doing her singing at all them theaters. You'll be all bleeding alone in that bloody big house, that's what."

Doris stamped her feet in frustration, furious that everyone seemed determined to crush her beautiful dream. "I don't care. I'll meet a toff, and I'll marry him and have a big house and lots of children." She glared at Daisy. "And I won't *be* a nanny; I'll have me own nanny to take care of me children. And I won't invite none of you to tea, so there.''

"So who bleeding cares?'' Gertie said rudely and began stomping off across the wet grass.

"I care!'' Doris cried. "I'm going to be famous, and no one is going to stop me.''

She felt a pat on her arm and looked around at Daisy, who stood there looking as if she were about to cry. "It's all right, Doris,'' she whispered. "You will be famous, and you'll meet a toff who wants to marry you. I just know it.''

Doris brushed back the tears threatening to fall. "Thank you, Daisy. I knew you'd understand. You can come to tea at my house when I get it.''

Daisy smiled. "I'd like that. Just as long as it ain't Lord Withersgill.''

Seated beside Madeline in the trap, Cecily felt a sense of profound despair. She forced herself to face the truth. The longer the delay in finding Phoebe, the worse the chance became of finding her alive. In spite of Madeline's conviction that Phoebe would be found at the vicarage, Cecily couldn't help feeling that it might well be Phoebe's dead body that had been recovered.

The trap bounced and lurched down the road to the village, and she was greatly relieved when they finally came to a halt. Apparently Algie and his weary helpers had also given up the search. They straggled past the trap in single file as Cecily alighted, barely glancing up as they trudged by.

Algie followed them, his glasses askew, the frail remnants of his hair ruffled above his ears. He still wore his cassock, the hem of which was torn and muddied. He stared bleakly and without hope at Baxter, who seemed unsure what to say to him.

"I don't suppose you've f-f-found her,'' Algie said in a voice so full of defeat and misery that Cecily's heart ached for him.

"I'm sure she'll be found soon," she said, praying that Madeline's prediction materialized.

Algie nodded and stumbled down the gravel path to the vicarage door, where the girls stood huddled by the steps. Cecily and Madeline followed, with Baxter bringing up the rear.

Algie produced a large iron key and fitted it into the ancient lock. "They've brought out the dogs," he said, twisting the key with some difficulty.

"Yes, we heard them." Cecily sought for something reassuring to add and could think of nothing.

"I saw the constables on the way back." A loud creak accompanied Algie's words as he pushed the door open. "They told me they were going to drag Deep Willow Pond. I don't know what they expect to find. Everyone knows the pond is bottomless. If mother is in there . . ."

His voice broke, and a rush of sympathy prompted Cecily to pat his shoulder. She was close to tears herself at the thought.

Algie's body shuddered as he took a deep breath. "Well, don't stand out there in the cold. Come inside and make yourselves warm. I'll put some milk on the stove—that's if it's still alight." His voice faded again. "Mother usually sees to these things."

"Baxter will light it if it's gone out," Cecily said kindly.

"Please be so good as to wait while I light the lamp," Algie muttered and disappeared into the darkness of the living room.

A moment or two later, a faint glow lit the neat, sparsely furnished drawing room, and Cecily stepped inside, followed by the rest of the subdued group.

Algie stood in the middle of the room, staring about him as if he wasn't sure where he was. The girls, still huddled together, crushed themselves into a corner of the room. Peeking into the kitchen next door, Cecily saw a thin line of glowing red embers. At least the stove was still alight and warming the house.

The flickering flame from the oil lamp threw strange shadows across the wall, dancing to the tune of Algie's shaking hand. Cecily could barely make out Baxter's face across the room in the dim light and was about to suggest that Algie turn up the wick when a sharp hiss made her turn her head.

The sound had come from the doorway leading to the stairs, and every head swiveled in that direction. Cecily's pulse leapt in horror when she saw the apparition in the doorway.

Ghostly white in the pale light from the lamp, it swayed back and forth, a frail hand fluttering at its breast. Even without the enormous brim of a hat, Cecily recognized the ethereal figure at once.

''Phoebe,'' she whispered, her lips cold with shock.

CHAPTER
❦ 17 ❦

"Mother!" Algie wailed at the precise moment that Cecily uttered her whispered exclamation.

"I thought as much," Madeline said smugly.

Baxter muttered something that was drowned by the belated shrieks of the girls, who had until now been frozen with terror.

First one, then another started screaming. Fragments of broken sentences burst from their open mouths, the gist of which appeared to be the conviction of the young ladies that they were in the presence of an evil spirit, namely that of Phoebe Carter-Holmes.

Cecily had been convinced herself for that matter, albeit just for a second or two. Then common sense had prevailed. Upon closer inspection, she could see quite clearly that Phoebe was very much alive, seemed every bit as shocked as everyone else, and was dressed solely in a voluminous white nightgown.

As far as Cecily could remember, in all the years she had known Phoebe, this was the very first time she'd seen her without her hat.

From where she stood, it was difficult to determine whether the wad of hair beneath the nightcap on Phoebe's head was actually a wig, which was the general consensus among the people well acquainted with the vicar's mother.

Unnerved by the shrill screams still erupting from the open mouths of the dance troupe, Cecily took hold of the nearest girl and shook her hard. She happened to have picked on Marion, the undisputed leader of the group.

Marion's teeth rattled as Cecily gave the shoulders of the heavily built girl another firm shake. At least the action had the desired effect. Marion shut her mouth and stopped screaming. Her eyes remained wide with fear, however, as she stared blankly across the room.

"What in the good Lord's name are you all doing in here?" Phoebe's shrill voice demanded above the hubbub. "Has everyone gone mad?"

One by one the girls fell mercifully silent.

"I . . . we apologize for disturbing you—" Baxter began when no one else seemed inclined to answer.

Phoebe stared at Baxter in horror, uttered a loud shriek, and disappeared.

"Mother!" Algie called out again and rushed after her. Everyone was silent as they listened to him pounding up the stairs.

"Well," Madeline said, "I suppose someone should tell the constables that there's no longer any need to search Deep Willow Pond."

"I'll be happy to oblige," Baxter said, sounding not at all happy at the prospect. "I suggest you ladies remain here until I return for you."

"I think that's a good idea." Cecily sank wearily into a shabby armchair. "I need to talk to Phoebe and find out exactly what happened."

Baxter turned to Madeline. "Before I leave, I believe

congratulations are in order." Without giving Madeline time to answer, he strode to the door and disappeared.

Cecily smiled at Madeline's look of confusion. "That was long overdue," she said smugly.

Madeline dismissed the moment with a quick shake of her head.

"I think I shall walk home," she said. "It isn't far, and I can accompany these young women on the way."

She walked to the door, ushering everyone ahead of her. The girls mumbled and muttered to each other but seemed only too happy to be going home to their beds.

Reaching the door, Madeline looked back at Cecily. "Tell Phoebe that I'm very happy she is unharmed."

Cecily sent her a tired smile. "Thank you, Madeline. I'm sure she'll be pleased to hear that."

For several minutes after Madeline had closed the door, Cecily rested alone in the peaceful silence. She was too tired even to think. The physical and emotional upheaval had taken their toll, and she had begun to doze when a rustling sound from the doorway brought her sharply awake again.

Phoebe swept into the room, wearing a dashing kimono of Japanese crêpe in Alice blue with a small Persian overall design that was most becoming.

She still wore her white, lace-trimmed nightcap, which looked slightly incongruous in Cecily's opinion. She was so happy to see her friend alive and well, however, she wouldn't have cared if Phoebe had worn nothing more than a flour sack on her head.

"I am so very sorry we disturbed you," she said when Phoebe perched herself on an ottoman. "I'm afraid it's largely my fault. I completely misjudged the situation."

Phoebe huffed out her breath. "Well, I must admit you gave me quite a fright. I couldn't imagine why everyone was in my drawing room, making so much ghastly noise."

"The girls thought you were an evil spirit, risen from the dead." Cecily shook her head in disbelief. "I can't imagine how I could have been so irresponsible.''

"Don't be so harsh on yourself, Cecily. Algie told me how everyone rallied around to join in the search for me. Most gratifying, I must say. I had no idea so many people cared about me.''

"We all care about you a great deal. In fact, Madeline asked me to tell you that she is very happy you are alive and well.''

"Really?'' Phoebe looked pleased. "How very gracious of her.''

"We were all extremely worried about you. Everyone was convinced that you had disappeared the same way that Ivy Glumm vanished, and we were all terribly concerned that you might end up in the same predicament.''

Phoebe nodded. "So Algie told me. What I don't understand is why you and everyone else assumed I had vanished. Algie was too exhausted to explain. I simply had to put the dear man to bed.''

"It was actually Colonel Fortescue who told us you had disappeared.'' Cecily hid a yawn by her hand. "Oh, please, excuse me.''

Phoebe looked puzzled. "Colonel Fortescue? Why would he think that?''

"He saw you step inside the magician's box on the stage. When you didn't come out again, he went to investigate. He opened the door and you had . . . vanished.''

"Oh, my.'' Phoebe pressed the tips of her fingers to her mouth. "I had no idea anyone had seen me.''

"Unfortunately the constable saw the colonel on the stage and arrested him. Since neither of them saw you leave the stage, the constable assumed that Colonel Fortescue was responsible for your disappearance.''

"Oh, the poor man. How very dreadful for him. I had no idea I had caused so much trouble.''

"Phoebe.'' Cecily leaned forward and peered intently at her friend. "How did you manage to get out of the box and, for that matter, out of the hotel without anyone seeing you?''

Phoebe's cheeks turned pink, and she looked most uncomfortable. ''I'm afraid I can't tell you that, Cecily. I have been sworn to secrecy. I have, in fact, sworn on my dead husband's grave that I would not reveal the secret of Denmarric's box. I cannot in all consciousness break that vow.''

Cecily shook her head. ''You won't have to reveal the secret to me, Phoebe, since I already know how the illusion was done. I examined the box myself and discovered the secret compartment at the rear of the box. It is opened by pressing the carved rose. Most ingenious, I might add.''

Phoebe looked horrified. ''You didn't tell anyone else, did you? I wouldn't want Charlotte Watkins to think that I had told you.''

Cecily frowned. ''How does Charlotte know you discovered the secret?''

''She was there when I stepped out of the back of the box.'' Phoebe shuddered. ''I found the secret catch quite by accident. In fact, if you hadn't mentioned the carved rose, I would never have known that was how it worked. I was prodding around in the dark, and all of a sudden the wall disappeared.''

''So you stepped out of the box and saw Charlotte?''

''I saw her standing right there in the wings. She stared at me and . . . she held a pistol aimed straight at my heart.''

Cecily jerked upright. ''A pistol?''

Phoebe nodded. ''The mere sight of that ugly thing pointed at me terrified me so much . . . why, I simply fainted dead away.'' She flapped a hand weakly in the air as if trying to dismiss the memory. ''I felt quite sure the dreadful woman was going to kill me.''

Could it have been Charlotte, after all, who had killed her husband's lover? Somehow Cecily didn't think so.

''Anyway,'' Phoebe continued, ''I woke up a short while later to find Charlotte Watkins hovering over me. At first it was almost enough to stop my heart altogether, until she began to apologize.''

"She apologized?''

"Yes. The pistol was actually a stage prop, you see. Apparently Charlotte had meant only to frighten me into promising to keep her husband's secret of the box. When I fainted dead away like that, she became quite concerned, fearing she'd harmed me in some way.''

"I see,'' Cecily said slowly. "Did she tell you why she was backstage or how she got there indeed, considering the area was under guard?''

"Charlotte told me she had gone backstage to collect some very important props for Mr. Denmarric's next performance. She was afraid they wouldn't be released in time. Apparently the props have to be primed before the actual performance, whatever that means.''

"And how did she manage to get there without being apprehended by the constable?''

Phoebe smiled. "Why, the same way I did, I imagine. The constable has a convenient habit of falling asleep, no doubt from boredom. After all, it must be simply dreadful to sit there all those hours with nothing to do but watch an empty stage. I can quite see how easy it would be for the poor man to fall asleep.'' She yawned delicately. "I must confess, I'm feeling quite sleepy myself.''

"I'm sorry, Phoebe. I'll leave as soon as Baxter comes for me.'' Cecily looked around for a clock and spied one on a table by the window. It was almost half past two. It would be dawn before she got back to the hotel if Baxter didn't return soon.

"Where did he go?''

"He went to inform the police you had been found. They intended to search Deep Willow Pond. He wanted to save them the trouble.''

"Oh, dear,'' Phoebe murmured.

"I do have one last question. How did you manage to leave the stage and the hotel without being seen?''

"Ah, well, after I promised Charlotte I would keep her secret, we left by the door into the ballroom. We couldn't allow the constable to see us, of course, since we weren't supposed to be there. When I opened the door, I saw the constable on the stage, talking to the colonel. Neither one of them noticed us slip out of the ballroom. I'm very light on my feet, you know, and Charlotte is a dancer."

"And you met no one on the way out?"

"Well, we left by the French windows and went through the rose garden, so we didn't have to pass through the hotel at all. Charlotte didn't want anyone to see her carrying all those props."

"I see."

"Of course, had I known that the colonel had seen me disappear, so to speak, and would raise the alarm, I would certainly have made my presence known. Though I must confess, I'm a little surprised that anyone paid him any heed."

"He was very convincing," Cecily said dryly. "His deep concern for your safety was indisputable."

"I've caused quite a stir, haven't I?" Phoebe said, sounding not in the least perturbed by the fact.

"Everyone thought you were whisked away by evil spirits, just like Ivy Glumm. The colonel was devastated. He'll be greatly relieved to know that you are safe, I know. He was quite beside himself with worry."

Phoebe actually blushed. "Indeed?" she murmured. "How interesting."

"Algie was most distraught, also. Even your dancers were concerned enough to join in the search."

"Most kind of them. I shall have to thank them personally when I see them. As for Algie, had he been here when I arrived home, instead of dawdling around the church for so long, none of this would have taken place. As it was, I decided to retire early and promptly fell asleep, or I would have been the one worrying about where he had been all night."

"I'm not sure how we are going to explain all this to the police without revealing Denmarric's secret." Cecily sighed. "I suppose I shall have to pay him another visit tomorrow and tell him what happened. I'm afraid his vanishing act will have to be revised."

"It is a pity," Phoebe murmured. "It was such a wonderful illusion. Yet so simple when you know how it is done. Isn't it amazing how easily one is fooled by illusion? Because Ivy Glumm had vanished from that box, everyone assumed that I had, too. No one questioned the fact enough to at least take the time to see if I was at home."

"I admit we all took a great deal for granted." The sound of horse hooves crunching on the gravel outside signaled Baxter's return at last. "But one thing I do know," Cecily said, fighting back another yawn, "is that Ivy Glumm's death was no illusion. I believe that someone waited for her in the wings that night, someone who was responsible for her death."

"I wonder if we shall ever know how she died. I'm beginning to think we shall have Mr. Denmarric's props cluttering up the stage forever."

"If only I could discover who it was backstage that night with Ivy." Cecily paused, listening to Baxter's footsteps approaching the door. "You are quite certain, Phoebe, that you saw no one when you went to the wings that night?"

"Only that insolent stagehand," Phoebe said. "But he couldn't have been the one laughing back there. I'm quite sure that whoever was responsible for that dreadful laughter was a woman."

Cecily straightened with a start. She had quite forgotten about the laughter.

"It was such a ghastly sound," Phoebe said, shivering. "I shall never forget it. I know it must have been the murderer making that awful noise. After all, I hardly think that Ivy would be laughing if someone was trying to kill her."

Cecily stared at Phoebe, the words repeating slowly in her mind.

Just then the door opened, and Baxter put his head inside. "I had imagined you would be sound asleep by now," he observed.

"As a matter of fact," Cecily said, rising to her feet, "Phoebe and I have been having quite a stimulating conversation."

Stimulating enough, she silently added, that she just might have the answer as to how Ivy had died.

If she was right, then she also knew the identity of the person who had killed the young woman and buried the body deep in the woods on Putney Downs.

CHAPTER 18

Samuel whistled as he crossed the courtyard to the kitchen door the next morning. In spite of his lack of sleep, he felt in remarkably good spirits. He'd finally made up his mind what he wanted to do about Doris. He'd thought long and hard about his decision, and the more he thought about it, the more certain he was that he'd be doing the right thing.

The big problem now, of course, was to persuade Doris that it was the right thing to do. No easy task, if he knew Doris. She'd probably give him all sorts of reasons why it wasn't a good idea.

He lifted his chin as the fresh breeze tugged at his cap. He loved this time of year in Badgers End. He could hear the birds whistling and chirping in the sycamore trees, feeding hungry mouths and encouraging the little ones to fly, as they did every year around this time.

The breeze from the sea had lost its chill, warmed by the sun that glistened on the white walls of the Pennyfoot Hotel. The hotel had been home for Samuel ever since he was a nipper, sent out into the world to earn some money for his starving, fatherless family up north.

The youngest of his siblings had left home a while ago, and his mother had married again. Now Samuel was responsible for only himself, and the world was his to explore and discover. Until now he'd been content to stay right where he was, among people he knew and trusted, secure in the knowledge that he would always have a warm bed, food in his stomach, and a bit of change to enjoy a pint down the George and Dragon when he fancied it.

Samuel reached the kitchen door and paused, his hand on the latch. Now things were different. It was time to strike out—to see the world and find out where adventure might lead him. He knew exactly the direction he wanted to take—and with whom he wanted to take it. All he had to do was convince her of that.

The fragrant, moist heat of the kitchen greeted him when he opened the door. Doris was in her usual spot in front of the sink, arms buried in hot, steaming water to the elbows. She turned her head to look at him as he walked in, and he thought he'd never seen a more lovelier picture.

Her cap sat on top of her light brown curls, and a dot of white foam caressed her flushed cheek. Her eyes sparkled at him as she greeted him with a wave of a soapy arm. "Your pasty's in the oven," she called out. "Help yourself."

He nodded and pulled off his cap, stuffing it into his pocket as he marched across the red tile floor to the stove. "I'll stoke it up for you," he offered. "It's getting a bit low."

"Thanks, Samuel." The clatter of plates almost drowned out her words.

Samuel shoveled more coal into the greedy mouth of the stove and closed the door. The pasty was hot when he grabbed it off the tray, and he hissed when it burned his fingers. Tossing it from one hand to the other he dashed over to the table and dropped it onto the scrubbed surface. The meaty, onion smell of it stirred pangs of hunger in his stomach.

Even so, he let it cool there while he sauntered casually over to the sink. Leaning his back against the draining board, he said softly, "So, how are you this morning, Bright Eyes?"

"Tired." Doris passed a soapy hand across her brow, leaving a trail of frothy suds. "I didn't get more'n an hour's sleep last night. Daisy kept talking about Lord Withersgill and kept me awake."

"I reckon we'll all be dragging our feet today." Samuel plucked a soap bubble from the sink and blew it gently into the air. It wafted over to Doris and settled on her cap, a clear, colorful, fragile thing that would vanish at the slightest touch.

That's how he felt about Doris, he thought, watching her lift the china plates and stack them onto the draining board one by one. One false step and she could vanish from his life forever. He had to be careful how he told her what was on her mind.

"You eaten your pasty already?"

He started, unaware that she'd been staring at him. "Not yet. I thought I'd let it cool off a bit."

"You all right? You're awfully quiet. Usually you don't shut up talking."

He grinned. "I'm tired, that's all. I didn't sleep good neither, what with getting to bed so late after all that excitement. I had so many thoughts going through my mind, I just lay there and listened to them."

His heart thumped for a minute. This was his opportunity to tell her what was on his mind. "Doris—"

"Well, I'm just glad they found Mrs. Carter-Holmes. I don't know her that well, but I wouldn't want her to end up the same way as that poor Ivy Glumm."

Disappointment took his breath away. He'd hoped that at least she would ask him what he'd been thinking about all night. "Yeah, it's good that they found her. Though I do think she might have told someone she was all right before she went home, instead of everyone thinking the murderer had done her in and having us all out there all night looking for her."

Doris smiled. "It were a bit of an adventure, though, weren't it? Fancy meeting Lord Withersgill like that. Real exciting, that were."

"Yeah, well, you'll be getting all the excitement you want when you go to London," Samuel said, trying to sound offhand. Inside he was quivering with apprehension.

"I know." Doris lifted her face and closed her eyes. "Just think, this time next week I'll be on me way to London for me audition. My whole life could be changed in one day."

Now! Samuel urged himself. *Say it now!* He cleared his throat. "Doris—"

The door flew open with a resounding smack against the wall, and Gertie rushed in, cap on askew and strands of her black hair falling across her eyes. "Strewth! I bleeding overslept. I didn't even have time to help get the flipping babies dressed this morning. Daisy'll have her hands bleeding full, I can tell you."

Samuel gritted his teeth but managed a faint grin. "Don't worry. I won't tell no one."

"Bleeding good job and all," Gertie snapped. "I'd soon tell a few bloody stories of me own about a certain stable manager what spends his time hanging around the kitchen instead of mucking out the stables."

"I haven't eaten my pasty yet." Samuel reached for the warm pie and bit into it. The tender morsels of beef, onion, and potato melted in his mouth and warmed his stomach.

"Bleeding spoiled you are," Gertie grumbled as she grabbed up the tray of clean silverware and headed for the door. "Mrs. Chubb don't let us eat anything between meals unless it comes back from the dining room."

"Ah," Samuel said with a wink, "you have to know

how to butter the old girl up. Takes a man to do that.''

Gertie laughed. "Yeah? Well, when you see one, let me know." The door swung to behind her, leaving him alone with Doris again.

Determined to get out what he wanted to say before he was interrupted again, Samuel went back to the sink. "Doris, I came to a decision last night. I've decided to look for a better job."

Doris gave him a startled glance. "I thought you was happy here."

"Well, I am . . . but I can't be a stableman all me life. I have to go on to bigger and better things."

"Like what?"

"Well . . ." He took a big breath. "I'd like to drive a delivery van. I'm good with horses, and I thought I might drive for one of the breweries. Someone I met down the George and Dragon told me as how they make really big money."

Doris laid a plate down on the draining board and wiped the soapsuds from her arms. "I didn't know there was any breweries near here."

"There isn't." Samuel could feel his throat closing up and swallowed hard. "Well, what I thought was, seeing as how you might be living in London, I thought I might go up there, too. I could earn a lot more money, and maybe we could see each other . . . only when you had the time, of course," he added hastily when Doris gave him a dark look. "I just thought it might be nice for you to have someone up there you knew, that's all. You never know when you might need a friend."

"Bella DelRay is my friend," Doris said, reaching for the tea towel. She began wiping the soapy water off the plates with it.

"Well, I know that. But she's really famous, and I reckon she's busy a lot of the time, traveling around and everything."

"Daisy said she might come up, too," Doris said stubbornly.

Feeling a little desperate, Samuel strived not to sound too eager. "Well, that'd be really nice for you if she did. But what if she didn't? What if she decides to stay here and look after Gertie's babies?"

Doris appeared to give that some serious thought. Then she laid down the plate and turned to him. "Samuel, I've been thinking, too. It could be lonely up there in a big city, all by meself. I don't really know Bella DelRay all that well, though she's really, really nice. I think it would be very nice to have a friend up there that I could see . . . just now and again, of course. When I'm not too busy on the stage, like."

"Of course!" He'd practically shouted the words, he was so chuffed. "Maybe we could go to Kew Gardens or see Buckingham Palace."

Doris's eyes grew wide. "Oo, can we see the Tower of London?"

Samuel nodded, feeling as if he would burst with joy and relief. "And London Bridge and the Embankment and Big Ben—"

"And we can go rowing on the Serpentine in Hyde Park." Doris clapped her hands, jumping up and down in her excitement. "We might even see the suffragettes get arrested."

"We might even see the king."

"Oh, Samuel, it's going to be so much fun."

His throat was so tight, he could hardly speak. He just looked at her and nodded. This had to be the very best moment of his life. If he lived to be a hundred, he would never forget standing in the warm, cozy kitchen of the Pennyfoot Hotel with the sun streaming through the windows, watching Doris in her too-big apron gazing at him with such a glow of excitement on her lovely face.

•　•　•

Cecily entered the waiting room of Dr. Prestwick's surgery, relieved to find that only three patients had arrived before her. She was anxious to talk to the doctor, and she didn't have much time. If he told her what she hoped he'd tell her, there might still be time to clear up this murder so that the tea dance could go on as planned.

There was another urgent reason she needed to see him, however, that took precedence over everything else. That reason had her fidgeting with impatience until at last Emily, Dr. Prestwick's assistant, called her name to enter his office.

Kevin Prestwick looked up as she entered the room, a frown marring his face. "Are you ill, Cecily?"

"No, Kevin, I'm not." She sat herself down on the deep leather arm chair. "I've come to ask you one or two questions."

He looked at her with disapproval in his eyes. "If it's about the murder, I've told you everything I know."

Cecily balanced her parasol against the chair leg. "As a matter of fact, I've come about an employee of mine, Ethel Salter."

Prestwick's face closed up. "You know I can't discuss my patients with you. Not without their permission, in any case."

"I realize that. I'm not asking you to jeopardize your integrity." Cecily folded her hands in her lap. "As a matter of fact, I've come to inform you of something I think you should know. Mrs. Chubb tells me that Ethel is refusing to go to a sanitarium for treatment for her consumption."

"I see." The doctor sat back in his chair and began tapping his teeth with a pencil. "How did your housekeeper find out about that?"

Cecily smiled. "There isn't much that escapes the grapevine at the Pennyfoot. Gertie was with Ethel when she told Joe she wasn't going to leave him. Gertie told Mrs. Chubb, who informed me."

Prestwick nodded, his face serious. "It is true Ethel refuses to leave her home. I have tried to persuade her otherwise, but to no avail. As I'm sure you know, without treatment, Ethel probably will not live out the year.''

Cecily did her best to hide her tremor of fear. ''Madeline has offered her home for Ethel's convalescence, which means she would be away for only a short while. I think if she knows that she might reconsider. Since Mrs. Chubb was anxious that Ethel should not find out that Gertie told her about her condition, I would be grateful if you would give Ethel the news of Madeline's generous offer.''

Prestwick stared at her in silence for a long time. Then he said softly, ''Miss Pengrath is a remarkable woman indeed.''

''Yes, she is. And if more people took the time to know her, they would discover just how remarkable. She is not the wicked witch most people imagine her to be.''

The doctor's lips twitched. ''Miss Pengrath does not believe in modern medicine. We had a heated discussion about it the last time we met, if I remember correctly. I don't think she would appreciate me attempting to become better acquainted with her.''

Cecily raised her eyebrows. ''Why, Kevin, I wasn't suggesting that you pursue her. I merely wanted to point out that Madeline is more than capable of taking care of Ethel once she has completed her treatment.''

Prestwick's expression sobered. ''You are aware, of course, that even with treatment Ethel might not recover.''

''I am aware, yes. That doesn't mean I accept it.'' Cecily straightened her back. ''I have long been under the impression that to think positively is to achieve success. I believe Ethel will get well. Even so, I want her to have the best chance possible.''

Prestwick nodded. ''Very well. I accept Miss Pengrath's kind offer. I hope that I can persuade Ethel to agree.''

''If you explain to Joe that Ethel will die if she doesn't go, I think he will be able to persuade her. I don't think he realizes that yet.''

"Don't worry, Cecily. I'll see that she goes."

Cecily relaxed her shoulders, content now to leave the matter in his capable hands. "Thank you, Kevin. I know you will do your very best. Now, if I may, I have one more question."

"Very well. What else can I do for you?"

"I would like some information on the effects of laughing gas. The kind the dentists use on their patients."

Prestwick studied her with narrowed eyes. After a moment or two he said slowly, "Nitrous oxide is an anesthetic, used by dentists to dull the pain and give the patient a feeling of well-being, often producing involuntary laughter."

"Yes, so I believe." Cecily leaned forward. "What I want to know is what actually happens when someone inhales the gas."

The doctor's frown deepened. "The gas depresses the central nervous system."

"Could it be fatal?"

"As long as it is used in conjunction with oxygen, the gas is quite safe."

"And if it's used without?"

Prestwick sighed. "If used without oxygen, nitrous oxide would certainly be lethal within seconds."

"And the heart would stop beating."

"To all intents and purposes," Kevin Prestwick said with a look of growing enlightenment, "the patient would essentially suffocate."

"Could Ivy Glumm have suffocated in that manner?"

Prestwick threw down his pencil. "By heaven, Cecily, you are magnificent. That could very well be the cause of Ivy's death. I just never thought of her being administered gas."

"What's more, I believe I know who killed her. Denmarric sacked his previous assistant, a young woman by the name of Jasmine Hicks, in order to hire Ivy. Although Jasmine did her best to hide it when we talked, she's very bitter, especially since Denmarric apparently ruined her reputation so that she can't get any more work on the stage.''

"Then why did she kill Ivy? Why not Denmarric?"

Cecily shrugged. "Jasmine is more likely to blame Ivy than the magician. Besides, with Ivy out of the way, there's always the chance that Denmarric would hire her back."

Dr. Prestwick played with the pencil on his desk, a brooding look on his face. "Hmm, I suppose that could be it. I assume that Jasmine, if she did do it, would have to use the dentist's equipment. How would she get it to the hotel, though, without being seen?"

"She could have easily brought it in through the rose garden earlier and hidden it there. I have no gardener at present, and it's unlikely the equipment would be discovered. All she had to do then was use the props basket to transport it backstage, dressed as a stagehand, of course."

"And she left with Ivy's body the same way?"

"Probably after everyone had left the ballroom. Most likely she hid the body until she could remove it unseen. It wouldn't be that difficult. Ivy was quite tiny, and there are lots of places to hide a body beneath costumes or behind backdrops."

Prestwick nodded. "What about the constable left on guard?"

"I understand he had a tendency to fall asleep while on duty."

"That doesn't surprise me."

"In any case, I think I shall make another appointment with the dentist."

Prestwick looked apprehensive. "That might not be wise, Cecily. In any case, your theory would be most difficult to prove. Wouldn't it be better to let Inspector Cranshaw deal with it?"

"Undoubtedly, but it will take him considerable time to conduct his investigation. I don't have that much time."

She rose, and the doctor rose with her, his face creased with anxiety. "What do you intend to do, Cecily?"

She smiled. "I'm not really certain of that, Kevin. But I can assure you I'll think of something."

CHAPTER

❈ 19 ❈

"Just look at these spring greens," Mrs. Chubb said, waving the bunch of dark green leaves at Gertie in disgust. "There's not one leaf that hasn't been half eaten by slugs. Disgusting, if you ask me, what with the price that greengrocer charges for them."

Gertie nodded in sympathy, her fingers straying to the letter in her pocket. Ross's last letter had contained such exciting news, she was afraid she was going to wake up and find out she dreamt it.

"I don't know what we're going to do if Mr. Baxter doesn't find a gardener soon," Mrs. Chubb grumbled. "How are we supposed to give our guests good food if we can't get decent produce from the greengrocer? Things just haven't been the same since John Thimble died. We always had good produce when he took care of the gardens."

Gertie's heart jumped so hard as the idea hit her that she almost forgot to breathe. Without letting herself think about it, she blurted out, "I know someone who could do the bleeding gardening."

Mrs. Chubb stared at her. "You do? Why didn't you say something before? You know madam and Mr. Baxter are having such trouble finding someone."

"Well, I didn't know until this morning." Gertie curled her fingers around the letter in her pocket, beginning to wish she hadn't been so hasty. What if she was doing the wrong thing? She hadn't really thought about it all that much.

"Well, go on with it, then. Who is it?"

"Well, I don't know if he'll want to do it, mind you, but . . . I think he might."

"So who is it, then?"

Gertie took a deep breath, and her words came out in a rush. "Ross McBride." She pulled the letter from her pocket as Mrs. Chubb's jaw dropped in astonishment. "He wrote in here as how he wants to come back to Badgers End to live. For a while, at least. He really liked it here, and he says he misses it so much."

Mrs. Chubb sniffed. "Misses you, you mean."

Gertie felt her cheeks grow warm. "Well, me, too, I s'pose. Anyhow, he says as how he'd have to find a job and somewhere to live, but I know he knows gardening 'cos he told me. Mind you, I don't know how bleeding good he is—"

"You're not thinking of getting married again, are you?" Mrs. Chubb demanded.

Gertie's heart felt as if it almost came out of her mouth. "What, me? Cor blimey, Mrs. Chubb, you know me better than that. I wouldn't bleeding get in bed with another man if me bloody life depended on it. Strewth, what you flipping take me for?"

Mrs. Chubb folded her arms across her ample bosom. "I take you for a young woman who has enough sense not to get tangled up with a man again unless she's very, very sure about him. You've got two young children to worry about now, you know.''

Gertie scuffed her toe on the tile floor. ''I ain't bleeding getting tangled up with no one, so you can stop bloody worrying. All I'm saying is, Ross McBride wants to live in Badgers End and needs a flipping job. We need a bleeding gardener. Makes blinking sense, don't it?''

Mrs. Chubb was silent for a long time, while Gertie waited in an agony of suspense. Finally she said quietly, ''I'll have a word with madam about it. But I'm not going to promise anything.''

''It don't make no bleeding difference to me, does it?'' Gertie stomped over to the dresser and opened the doors. Her hands shook so much that she could hardly hold the soup tureen she lifted off the shelf.

She'd bleeding done it now, she thought as she carried the huge bowl over to the stove. She'd started something she might not be able to bloody finish. Then again, even if Ross McBride did come back to Badgers End, that didn't mean she'd have to bleeding take up with him.

They was just friends, like she told him the last time she saw him. She'd told him she couldn't marry him, and she'd meant it. She'd have to make that bloody clear to him if he did take the job at the Pennyfoot.

Even so, her stomach felt like it was filled with squiggly worms. The very thought of the burly Scotsman right there in Badgers End made her feel faint at the thought. No one had ever made her feel the way he had.

''Come on, Gertie, stop your daydreaming and fill that tureen.''

Mrs. Chubb's voice snapped Gertie out of her daze. The housekeeper was right. The last thing Gertie Brown needed in her life was another man. She'd learned her lesson with the last one, and she wasn't about to bleeding forget it. Not even for Ross McBride.

• • •

"It was really so nice of the dentist to see me again without an appointment," Cecily said as Jasmine led her into the cubicle. "I wouldn't have bothered him, if I weren't having so much trouble with my teeth."

"You were lucky, Mrs. Sinclair. Dr. Rodgers wasn't very busy today," Jasmine explained as she took Cecily's hat from her and ushered her into the leather chair. She reached for a white bib and began tying it around Cecily's neck.

"This job must be so very different from your stage career," Cecily remarked pleasantly. "Did you find it difficult to get used to the change in your work hours? You must have to get up much earlier than you've been used to."

Jasmine shrugged. "One soon gets used to it. Now, if you'll just lie back, Mrs. Sinclair—"

"I often wonder what Denmarric will do now," Cecily went on as if she hadn't heard. "Ivy was such an asset to his act—I'm sure he'll miss her dreadfully."

Jasmine's mouth tightened. "If you don't mind, Mrs. Sinclair . . ."

"I watched her with him that last night. She was so quick on her feet and so attentive. It was almost as if she read his mind."

"Mrs. Sinclair—"

Pleased to note that Jasmine's voice had risen just a shade, Cecily went on, "I wonder if that's possible. You know, the assistant reading the magician's mind? I wouldn't be at all surprised. The way that young lady performed was nothing short of miraculous. Mr. Denmarric must be absolutely devastated. Quite lost without her, I should imagine. It would be very difficult to replace someone like that."

"Mrs. Sinclair!" Jasmine's face was contorted with fury. "I really don't wish to discuss Ivy Glumm. She was hopeless, utterly useless as an assistant to a magician like the Great Denmarric."

Cecily raised her eyebrows in feigned surprise. "Really?

I was under the impression he would have been helpless without her."

To Cecily's great satisfaction, this proved to be the last straw for Jasmine. She threw down the instrument tray she was holding with a sound of angry disgust. "That . . . that silly cow made so many mistakes, I'm surprised any of his illusions worked. Why, she was always handing him the wrong thing. You should have seen how furious he was the night he announced to the audience he was going to produce a dove and instead he pulled a duck out of his pocket. Can you imagine how embarrassing that was for him?"

"That's very interesting, Jasmine, " Cecily murmured. "How did you know about that incident?"

"I know that because I saw it," Jasmine cried, her cheeks flushed with anger. "I was standing right there—"

She broke off and stared in horror at Cecily.

"In the wings," Cecily finished for her. "That's what you were going to say, wasn't it, Jasmine? That incident with the duck happened the other night, when Denmarric was appearing at the Pennyfoot. The night Ivy was killed. And you were standing in the wings, waiting for her to come out of the box."

Jasmine shook her head violently. "No, that's not true. I wasn't there that night. I told you. Someone else must have told me about the duck. Lots of people were talking about it the next day."

"Oh, I think you were there that night, Jasmine." Cecily removed the bib from her neck. "I think you dressed up as a man, pretending to be a stagehand. They were the only people allowed backstage while Denmarric was setting up his act. You waited for Ivy to emerge from the box, then administered the gas. Ivy was slight, and you are quite strong, as you pointed out to me the last time I was here. It wouldn't have been too difficult for you to overpower her."

Jasmine shook her head again. "Mrs. Sinclair, I don't know what you are talking about. I—"

"The laughter everyone heard came from Ivy, just before she died," Cecily went on relentlessly. "You put her body into the props basket and wheeled her out to the wings, where you hid her until everyone had left the ballroom. I suspect that you then took the basket out to a trap left conveniently in a quiet spot, unloaded Ivy's body, then returned the basket before driving up into the woods."

Jasmine's face was now white, with two spots of red above her cheekbones. She clenched her hands, and her voice shook when she muttered, "You're talking a lot of twaddle, Mrs. Sinclair. I've never been near the Pennyfoot Hotel. Not that night, not ever."

Cecily shifted her position. "When I sat in this chair on my last visit, I happened to notice a flash of light reflecting off the gas machine over there. I'm quite certain that if we look closer, we'll find one or two of Ivy's silver sequins stuck there. Sequins from the costume she was wearing when she was murdered. A costume, I might add, that had been purchased especially for that performance."

Watching Jasmine's face, Cecily knew she had struck home. The assistant's eyes narrowed. Keeping her gaze fixed on Cecily, she moved over to the machine.

Before Cecily realized her intention, Jasmine grabbed the gas mask and with a swift movement clamped it hard over Cecily's mouth and nose.

Jasmine had been right about one thing. She was very strong. Cecily held her breath and fought to drag her face free from the mask, but to no avail. Jasmine held on tight, while the blood pounded in Cecily's head and stars danced in front of her eyes.

One by one those stars were fading, and she knew that any second now, she would have to take a breath. A breath of deadly gas. More than likely her last breath.

Phoebe arrived breathless at the top of the steps of the Pennyfoot and rang the bell. Ned opened the door and gave her an audacious wink. "Well, if it ain't the lovely lady herself. Thought you was a goner for sure. Had me best whistle all ready to pay me respects at the funeral and all.''

Phoebe spared him a look of disdain as she stepped past him into the foyer. "Why on earth would you want to take a whistle to a funeral?''

"Nah, mum, not a whistle. Whistle and flute—suit.''

Phoebe tossed her head. "Really!" She had no idea what the dreadful man was talking about, nor did she care to know. "Pray tell me, young man, where might I find Mrs. Sinclair?''

Ned closed the door, shaking his head. "You won't find her, mum. Least, not in here. She's off somewhere. Same as Mr. Baxter. He took off out of here soon after, like a dog after a hare. Never seen him move so fast before.''

Phoebe sighed. "Never mind. Actually I came to have a word with Colonel Fortescue. Can you tell me where he is?''

Ned looked astounded. "You want to talk to the colonel? Most people do their best to stay out of his way.''

"Well, I'm not most people. And you are being impertinent, young man." Phoebe glared at him. "Please answer my question. Where might I find Colonel Fortescue?''

"Well, mum, he's most likely in the drawing room, enjoying his spot of gin." Ned grinned. "I'd watch him if I were you, Mrs. Carter-Holmes. Our colonel can be a bit naughty when he's on the mother's ruin.''

"I am quite aware of the gentleman's shortcomings, thank you." Phoebe gave her hat a sharp tug with both hands, then squared her shoulders. "I shall go in search of him. Thank you, Ned.''

"My pleasure, mum. Good to see you safe and well. We was all worried about you last night.''

Phoebe huffed out a breath, pretending she wasn't at all flattered by the young's man concern. Hurrying down the long hallway, she rehearsed her speech, hoping that the colonel would still be responsive enough to understand her.

Colonel Fortescue sat alone in the drawing room, as

Phoebe expected, his face hidden behind a newspaper. The other guests rarely remained in the room with him for long, wary of being embroiled in one of the colonel's many stories about his life in the military.

The colonel's stories, as far as Phoebe's experience of them anyway, were invariably long-winded and more often than not somewhat offensive.

She paused in front of him and heard a faint snore from behind the newspaper. "Good afternoon, Colonel," she said loudly.

The snoring ceased, and he mumbled something unintelligible. Phoebe waited, but when he remained behind the newspaper, she leaned closer. "Good afternoon, Colonel!" she yelled.

The newspaper rattled violently, then fell, revealing the flushed face of the colonel. "I say, old girl, no need to shout, what? Scared me half to death. Could give a chap a heart attack, you know."

"I want to talk to you," Phoebe announced, unscathed by his reprimand.

As if suddenly remembering his manners, the colonel leapt to his feet, staggering a little before he grabbed the arm of the chair to steady himself. "Good to see you again, Mrs. Carter-Holmes." He swayed, fixing his bleary stare on her face. "I say, old girl, do you mind if I call you Phoebe? Bit long-winded between friends, all that Carter-Holmes stuff, what?"

Taken aback by this unexpected request, Phoebe lost her composure. "Oh, well, I don't know, I mean, well, I suppose it would be all right—"

"Jolly good show! That's settled, then. Well, Phoebe, what do you want to talk about?"

Phoebe did her best to collect herself. She seemed to have forgotten her well-prepared speech. "I . . . er . . . well, actually, I came to apologize."

"Oh, that's all right, old bean. I don't mind being woken up by such a charming lady as yourself, what?"

Phoebe blinked. "Woken up? Oh, no, I don't mean just now. I mean about last night. Yesterday. I understand that you had a rather trying experience with the police because of my disappearance. I suppose I should have told someone I was going home, but then I had no idea you were there watching me get into that silly box."

The colonel stared at her for several seconds, then startled her by slapping his hand down hard on the arm of the chair. "By George, I'd forgotten about that. Someone told me you were all right. Safe and sound in your own home, by Jove. That's why I was celebrating." He leaned forward, whispering loudly, "Would you care to join me, old bean? We can celebrate together."

Not sure she was following, Phoebe asked warily, "Celebrate what?"

"Why, your marvelous escape from those bastards, of course. Dashed fine bit of work, I must say. Don't know how you managed it, but I'm proud of you. It's not often someone gets out of their clutches."

Phoebe shook her head in bewilderment. "I haven't the faintest idea what you're talking about, Colonel."

"Well, no matter. Let me order you a drop of gin from the bar. Do you the world of good."

Remembering her last experience with the colonel's gin, Phoebe hastily declined. "It's the middle of the day, Colonel. Too early for me, I'm afraid, but thank you, anyway."

"Too early? Balderdash! It's never too early for a spot of mother's ruin. I'll get one for you."

"Thank you, Colonel, but no," Phoebe said firmly.

"Then how about a nice drop of sherry?"

"I don't think so. I'm really not—"

"It will warm the cockles of your heart, madam. Wait there, and I'll be back in a jiffy."

Phoebe sighed as the colonel ambled out the door and headed for the bar. That was probably the last she'd see of him for the rest of the day. Perhaps it had not been such a good idea to pay him a visit on the pretext of apologizing for her vanishing act. Perhaps she should have revealed her true reason for seeking his company.

The truth was she had been intrigued by Cecily's comments about the colonel's deep anxiety for her safety. Never one to miss an opportunity, Phoebe had decided that it would do no harm to find out just how deeply the colonel had been affected and whether, in fact, there might be some faint chance of something significant developing in that direction.

After all, from all accounts, Colonel Fortescue was quite wealthy. The fact that he was also quite potty could work in her favor. What the colonel obviously needed was a strong woman to handle his affairs, take over his household and servants, and generally make his life more pleasurable.

In return, Phoebe would have her long-sought security and a return to the life to which she was once accustomed. All in all a fair trade, she concluded.

Seating herself in the chair vacated by the colonel, Phoebe smiled to herself. She wondered what Cecily would say if she announced that she intended to marry Colonel Fortescue. No doubt everyone would think she was as mad as her prospective husband.

No, Phoebe thought, reaching for the newspaper. Cecily would understand. Cecily always understood. It was her compassion and sympathy that made her such a good friend.

Phoebe frowned, remembering Ned's words when she'd arrived. Cecily had gone somewhere, and Baxter had left soon after, apparently in a great hurry. Now that she came to think about it, Phoebe thought uneasily, that sounded rather ominous. She only hoped that Cecily wasn't in some kind of trouble.

Cecily, unfortunately, had a penchant for running into danger. Phoebe had often scolded her friend for her impulsiveness. One day, she'd warned, Cecily might very well encounter more trouble than she could handle. Phoebe could only hope that this latest emergency did not bear out her prophecy.

CHAPTER

❧ 20 ❧

Cecily heard a roaring sound in her ears as she struggled to loosen the deadly grip of Jasmine's strong fingers. Thoughts flashed through her mind in swift succession. Thoughts of Baxter and what he would say when her body was discovered. Would he mourn her, as he'd once mourned a young lost love, or would he be angry with her for again breaking her promise to advise him of her whereabouts? If she hadn't broken her promise, she wouldn't be in this predicament now.

I'm sorry, my dear love. Forgive me.

Michael. Andrew. How would her sons react to the news of her violent death? Would they come home for her funeral? Little James, the grandson she'd never see now. Her staff at the Pennyfoot, who had become her surrogate family. How shocked they would all be . . .

The roaring began to fade . . . she had to breathe . . . if she didn't she'd die anyway . . .

The explosion of sound seemed to come from a long way off. The pressure on her face was miraculously removed, and firm hands now grasped her shoulders.

"Breathe," Baxter's anguished voice ordered. "For God's sake, Cecily, breathe."

She tried, opening her mouth to gulp in the life-giving air. Sharp pains racked her chest and shoulders, and her head felt as if it had swollen like a rubber balloon.

She tried to speak but could manage only a whimper, her lungs striving, greedy for air.

"Help her to sit up," another voice commanded, and rough hands pulled her upright. She managed to open her eyes at last, and Baxter's face swam in front of her.

"Cecily, are you all right? How do you feel?"

"Stupid," she managed to gasp out.

Baxter's face seemed to crumple, and his arms closed around her with satisfying warmth. "Oh, my dear madam," he said brokenly.

Gradually the room stopped swirling around, and the pain began to subside in her chest. Drawing back from his embrace, she looked up into Baxter's face. He looked as if he'd aged since she last saw him, the lines in his face etched more deeply than she ever remembered.

"I'm sorry," she said unsteadily. "I should have told you. How did you know I was here?"

"You can thank the telephone for saving your life." Baxter let her go and straightened. "For once Prestwick showed some sense. He rang me after you left his office and told me you were coming here. He was concerned about your safety and felt that someone should be with you. He was right, of course. Had we not had that telephone put in, you would be dead by now."

Remembering Jasmine, Cecily looked across the room to where the girl sat on a chair, guarded by Dr. Rodgers, who seemed quite shaken. "I forgot the most important rule," Cecily murmured. "I underestimated the enemy."

"You also broke your promise to me," Baxter reminded her grimly.

"I'm sorry."

"I can't believe it," the dentist muttered. "To think that something like this could happen in my office. I just can't believe it."

"I asked Prestwick to ring the constable before I left," Baxter said as Cecily smoothed her hair with an unsteady hand. "He should be here shortly."

Jasmine seemed unperturbed by the news. She sat slumped in the chair, her hands tucked in the folds of her skirt and a stoic expression on her thin face.

She was so young, Cecily thought, with a pang of sympathy. One couldn't help feeling sorry for someone who had ruined her life before she'd really had a chance to live it. But then, she'd also taken a young life. "You must have hated Ivy very much," she said quietly.

Jasmine's slender shoulders lifted in a shrug, but she refrained from answering.

Feeling compelled to set things straight, Cecily tried again. "It wasn't really Ivy's fault, you know. If you had to blame someone for taking away your job, you should have blamed Denmarric. Ivy was weak, but not vindictive. It was Denmarric who threw you aside for Ivy Glumm, then persuaded you to murder her."

Cecily sensed Baxter's faint start of surprise. The dentist merely looked bewildered.

Jasmine stirred, then lifted her chin, her eyes filled with hate. "I did it for him," she said, her voice hard and bitter. "She was having his baby. He came to me and told me about it. He said she didn't mean anything to him. He said if I got rid of her, then I could go back to being his assistant."

"I thought as much," Cecily said, feeling a final sense of justification. "The magician planned it all, didn't he?"

Jasmine nodded. "He helped me set up the machine and ordered everyone away from the wings during the performance. Then, when everyone was gone, he helped me get her out of there and into the carriage.''

"Did he also help you bury her?''

"No. I did that by myself. He said it was safer that way.''

Cecily nodded. "Yes, I imagine it was safer for him.''

Jasmine's eyelids flickered, but she made no comment.

"How did you manage to get Ivy's body past the police guard?'' Baxter asked, his voice echoing his disgust.

Jasmine's gaze flicked across to his face for a second, then slid away. "Dennis kept the bobby talking backstage, while I took the basket out through the French doors.'' She stared at Cecily, her face looking old beyond its years. "Just like you said I did.''

Baxter muttered a quiet oath.

"No one would have found out, neither, if you hadn't seen those sequins on the machine.'' Jasmine started forward, and the dentist clamped his hand on her shoulder to hold her down. Narrowing her eyes, she directed a look of pure venom at Cecily. "You and your busybody poking into other people's business. If it wasn't for you, I would have been the Great Denmarric's assistant again, and everything would have been the same as it was before.''

"I don't think so,'' Cecily said, shaking her head. "I'm quite sure Denmarric would have found a way to get rid of you, just as he got rid of Ivy. Men like that only care about themselves. The act was all that was important to him. Nothing else. You got rid of Ivy for him, and now you will have to pay for it.''

Jasmine slumped back in her chair. "He'll pay, too,'' she muttered. "I'll see to that.''

Just then the door opened, and Inspector Cranshaw entered, followed closely by P.C. Northcott.

After several terse questions from the inspector were answered to his satisfaction, the constable led Jasmine away.

Just before he also left, Inspector Cranshaw lowered his dark brows and glowered at Cecily. "I would hope that this would be a lesson to you to stay away from police business in the future. Since I'm fully aware that the hope is futile, however, I will warn you once again of the consequences of intruding on territory where you have no business to be. You were lucky this time, Mrs. Sinclair. Believe me, as I have said before, one day that luck will run out, and you will be not be alive to hear me say I told you so.''

"Thank you, Inspector," Cecily said, deliberately avoiding Baxter's expression of complete accord. "I appreciate your concern, and I will take note of your warning."

With a look of skepticism on his face, the inspector left the room.

"Well, I don't know what to say," Dr. Rodgers said, wringing his hands. "I'm simply shocked by all this. I'm terribly sorry for what happened, Mrs. Sinclair. I sincerely hope this will not prevent you from seeking treatment for your teeth. As soon as I find a new assistant, that is.''

Cecily rose to her feet with the aid of Baxter's hand and reached for her hat. "Thank you, Dr. Rodgers. I'll be in contact with you later."

Still apologizing profusely, the dentist followed them to the door, and he still stood in the doorway, watching anxiously as they drove away.

Once they were out of the town, Cecily leaned back in the seat and drew in deep breaths, more appreciative than ever of the fresh, fragrant air. Sometimes one was inclined to take for granted the simple pleasures of life until she was threatened. Only then did one realize just how meaningful everyday life could be.

"Are you quite certain you feel well?" Baxter inquired as the chestnut settled down to an easy trot. "Perhaps we should call in on Prestwick and let him take a look at you."

"I'm quite all right," Cecily assured him. "Just a little shaken, that's all.''

Baxter sent her such a look of reproof she cringed. "I know what you're going to say," she said before he could speak. "And you are quite right. I behaved recklessly and

I was fortunate that you arrived in time to rescue me. I can assure you I will not break my promise to you again.''

He didn't look too convinced by her statement. ''Much as I hate to encourage you in this appalling avocation of yours, I must confess I'm curious as to how you identified Miss Hicks as the killer.''

Cecily gazed thoughtfully at the passing fields for a moment before answering. ''Actually it was the laughter. I had forgotten about that strange laughter we'd heard the night of the performance until Phoebe mentioned it again.''

Baxter frowned. ''I don't understand how that led you to Miss Hicks.''

''The last time I paid a visit to Dr. Rodgers, he kept me waiting. I heard laughter from another room, and when I mentioned it to Dr. Rodgers, he told me that he used laughing gas, which produces mild hysteria in some people. I asked Kevin Prestwick about it, and he told me it could be fatal if used improperly. That's when I knew how Ivy Glumm had died. The effects of the gas must have caused Ivy to laugh just before she died.''

The horse's hooves slowed as the trap drew up to a corner. Then Baxter flipped the reins, and they were off once again, passing hedges thick with the white blossoms of wild blackberries.

''But how did you know Denmarric had planned the murder?''

''I wasn't sure about that,'' Cecily admitted. ''It was more a shot in the dark. It just seemed strange to me that Denmarric would have had a spare costume for his wife with him that night. It couldn't have been one of Ivy's costumes, since it wouldn't have fitted Charlotte. She's gained quite a bit of weight since she was her husband's assistant. She admitted that herself. Therefore, Denmarric had to have a costume made especially for her, just as if he knew she would be appearing on stage that night.''

''Which he did know, of course.''

''Exactly. All that was carefully planned beforehand.''

"And the sequins on the gas machine that Miss Hicks mentioned?"

Cecily smiled. "Pure fabrication, I must confess. Jasmine wasn't admitting anything, in spite of my accusations, and I was afraid that I'd lost my opportunity to make her admit her guilt. I took a chance and invented the sequins in the hopes of shaking her composure. I succeeded."

"A little too well, I'd say," Baxter muttered.

Cecily sighed. "I must commend both Denmarric and Jasmine on their excellent acting. Denmarric looked stunned when he opened that empty box, and Jasmine looked just as shocked when I told her about Ivy's death."

"Well, both of them are stage personalities and well used to simulating expressions."

"Well, I was certainly fooled. As was everyone else. Denmarric won't get away with his part in it now, though, not with Jasmine's testimony against him."

"Cranshaw must have apprehended him by now."

"I suppose so. I wonder if Denmarric will be able to escape from prison."

Baxter looked amused by the thought. "I would hardly think so."

"Houdini could do it. He can escape from anything."

"Ah, but Denmarric is no Houdini."

Cecily smiled. "I suppose not. Nevertheless, I'd be inclined to take some precautions if I were a prison guard."

"What about George Dalrymple's dog? How did he get involved?"

"I think it was probably coincidence. George told me his dog often wandered off and was fond of the ladies. The dog probably formed a strong attachment to Ivy and just happened to be in the woods the night Jasmine buried her."

Baxter was silent, apparently deep in thought.

Cecily was content to sit there and listen to the steady clop of the chestnut's hooves, with the warm wind tugging at the scarf that anchored her hat and the solid comfort of Baxter's presence beside her.

• • •

Standing on the balcony overlooking the ballroom, Phoebe watched the women in their pretty pastel gowns gliding gracefully across the floor with their elegant partners. The tea dance was not one of her more ambitious presentations, and for that very reason she had high hopes of achieving a successful event for a change.

After all, what could possibly go wrong? Eleanor McAllister was a proficient pianist, and her voice was quite remarkable. Phoebe had been entranced throughout the soprano's performance in the church hall and was quite certain that she could well please this discriminating audience.

The lilting dance music came to a close, and the orchestra leader stepped up to center stage. "Ladies and gentlemen, I should like to introduce to you Miss Eleanor McAllister, a lady of remarkable talent, who will be pleased to entertain you with voice and piano."

A smattering of applause greeted the entry of a slender woman wearing an absolutely exquisite white gown, heavily embroidered and lavished with tucks and bands of lace. Phoebe clasped her hands at the sight, though it wasn't so much the gown that she envied as the magnificent hat the singer wore.

The wide, natural straw brim was almost hidden beneath two enormous white chrysanthemums, combined with purple and white pansies intermingled with pale green foliage. It utterly screamed Paris and had to have cost a small fortune.

Phoebe congratulated herself as the pianist seated herself in front of the Steinway and flexed her fingers. A beautiful picture indeed. Such a fitting introduction to the fashion presentation to follow. For once she would have a flawless performance.

Out of the corner of her eye, Phoebe noticed a small disturbance at the main doors of the ballroom. She paid little attention, however, since the pianist chose that mo-

ment to strike the dramatic opening chords of a Tchaikov-
sky piano concerto.

Enthralled with the crashing music echoing to the rafters,
Phoebe clasped her hands and prepared to be swept away.
Unfortunately, little ripples of noise from the audience un-
dermined the mesmeric effects of the pianist's efforts.

Frowning, Phoebe tore her gaze away from the magnificent creature at the piano and glared down at the offending
guests below. There appeared to be some kind of urgent
discussion going on. People were whispering, shaking their
heads, muttering to each other.

Phoebe's consternation grew when she saw two women
actually weeping. Surely there couldn't be another tragedy
at the Pennyfoot? Was the wretched hotel cursed, for
heaven's sake?

Watching the crowd below, it finally occurred to Phoebe
that too many people by far were being affected by the
news, whatever it was, for it to be simply another setback
for the hotel. By now the entire audience had abandoned
all pretense of listening to the pianist, who was still crashing out chords, oblivious of the tumult going on behind
her.

The members of the orchestra, however, who were facing
the ballroom floor, seemed to have been affected by the
same urgency as the rest of the room. One by one they
ceased playing, leaning toward each other to exchange
comments.

Phoebe felt like howling. Not again. How could this be
happening to her again? After all she'd been through, working so hard to get all those dreadful props off the stage in
time for this event.

Seething with frustration, she spotted Cecily standing by
the doors, apparently looking for someone. Without wasting
another second, Phoebe flew to the stairs and scurried down
them.

She had to fight her way past gesturing men and weeping

women, her apprehension rising as it dawned on her that this must be a major tragedy.

With one hand firmly clutching her hat, the other impatiently pushing aside whoever had the temerity to stand in her way, she finally arrived at the doors of the ballroom. Cecily had vanished, but one of the housemaids, Doris or Daisy, whichever one it was—Phoebe never could tell them apart—had just emerged from the ballroom carrying a tray of sherry glasses.

Phoebe grasped the girl's arm and pulled her aside. "Whatever is going on in there?" she demanded. "What's all the fuss about?"

The girl looked at her with wide eyes. "It's the king, mum," she said, so softly Phoebe had to strain to hear. "He died this morning. King Edward is dead."

"Mercy me!" Phoebe clutched her lace-bound throat, feeling as if she'd just fallen into the cold waters of Deep Willow Pond. "The king is dead?"

"Long live the king!" a familiar voice bellowed in her ear.

Spinning around, Phoebe looked into the florid face of Colonel Fortescue. "Well, old bean," he said, waving a half-filled glass in her face, "England has just got itself a new king. What do you blasted well think of that?"

Phoebe drew herself up. "Drat the man," she said, glaring back at him. "Couldn't he have waited just one more day?"

Cecily leaned across the half-barrel standing in the corner of the roof garden and nipped off a dried-up rosebud. "It seems as if we are to have a new gardener, after all," she commented, straightening to look at Baxter. "It's strange how things work out, don't you think?"

"I'll tell you what I think after he's worked here for a few months," Baxter said dryly. "After all, gardening is not his profession."

Cecily smiled. "Ross McBride is a good man, by all

accounts. I've often said that gardening is mostly a matter of good sense, in any case. I'm sure he will do well here. Though I am concerned about the sorry state of the grounds. I'm afraid he will have a great deal of work on his hands when he first arrives.''

''I suppose that any gardener is better than none. It would be impossible to find someone as efficient as John Thimble, I imagine.''

''Ross is a lot younger and stronger than was John. What Ross lacks in finesse he'll make up for in strength and endurance.'' Cecily looked around the bedraggled roof garden, so lovingly created by her late husband. ''I know that the lawns and shrubs of the main grounds must take priority, but I do long to have this garden up here renovated and established.''

''Perhaps I can give McBride a hand to construct it,'' Baxter offered, sounding excessively nonchalant.

''Oh, Bax, would you? I'd really love it.''

He looked pleased. ''I'll see what I can do.''

She turned from him and walked to the wall, where she could see across the bay to the thatched cottages in the village. ''It's hard to believe that King Edward has passed on. His death is bound to bring changes.''

Baxter came up and stood close behind her. ''Isn't that what you've been telling me for years, that life is full of changes, and that's the price we must pay for progress?''

She sighed. ''I suppose so. Sometimes I think you were right, though, and that the changes are happening too fast. Doris will be off to London soon, possibly to stay. Daisy might very well go with her. Ethel has already left for the sanitarium. That leaves only Gertie and Mrs. Chubb. What will Gertie do if Daisy leaves? What will happen to the Pennyfoot if we can't replace the girls?''

''We'll manage, the way we always have.''

She leaned back, seeking the comfort of his arms. ''It's not just our little world of Badgers End, Baxter. It's the whole country. There's so much talk of war in Europe, social unrest in all the big cities, women laying down their lives for privileges to which they should be entitled, and now we have reached the end of the Edwardian era. I have an uneasy feeling that a way of life is about to vanish into history.''

"It's the way of the world, my dear madam, as you are so fond of reminding me." His arms folded around her, drawing her close. "I think I can promise you this, Cecily. As long as we have the Pennyfoot, we have a home and security. And as long as we are together, our happiness is assured. We can't ask for much more than that."

"Indeed we can't, Baxter." In spite of her underlying apprehension, she tilted her head for his kiss, her heart in full agreement. For now, Baxter and the Pennyfoot were all she needed. She'd worry about the rest of it if and when it happened.